Ash woke up before her eyes opened. They felt gluey and tingly, like someone had taped them shut with Post-it notes. It took her a moment to rewind her memory enough to catch all the important facts. Her name was Ashley Arthur. She was fifteen. She lived with her dad at 146 East Park Way. She was a thief.

And the last thing that she remembered was driving a Bugatti Veyron off the roof of Hammond Buckland Solutions headquarters.

MONEY RUN

JACK HEATH

USBORNE

For Paul, my accomplice.

Also advisor, confidant and loyal friend

First published in the UK in 2011 by Usborne Publishing Ltd., Usborne House, 83–85 Saffron Hill, London EC1N 8RT, England. www.usborne.com

First published in 2008. Text copyright © Jack Heath, 2008

A CIP catalogue record for this book is available from the British Library.

ISBN 9781409531081 JFMA JJASOND/11 02240/1

Printed in Reading, Berkshire, UK.

Prologue

Don't get caught.

The girl's instinct was to move now. Screw the preparation. Screw the plan. Come up with something new, quickly. She was running out of time.

The fluorescent lights on the walls and ceiling of the cabin had been switched off – the gloom inside the plane was only occasionally pierced by the reading lamps of individual passengers. The roaring of the engines outside was dulled to a muted hum. The flight attendants had given out drinks and snacks, come back to take the wrappers away, and now sat in their seats up the front.

By the girl's watch, the plane was due to land in nineteen minutes. Which meant the descent would start in thirteen minutes. Which meant the captain would switch on the seat-belt sign in nine or ten minutes. Lights up, tray tables up, seats upright. Everything up as the plane goes down. All the other passengers would awaken, and buckle themselves in.

She had slipped a diuretic into passenger 8C's sparkling wine thirty-eight minutes ago, when she asked him if he had finished with his business magazine. The guy had given it to her, and sipped his drink without a hint of suspicion. But he still hadn't gotten up to go to the toilet.

She wanted to move now. Find another way to get the passenger out of seat 8C. Do what she needed to do, and get back to her row before the captain switched on the seat-belt sign. But she knew that changing the plan slashed her chances of success to almost nothing. Backing out was better than getting caught.

"We have to abort," the boy said. He seemed anxious. Like always, she thought.

She resisted the temptation to touch the tiny flesh-coloured speaker in her ear. "Not yet," she said.

The boy was sitting five rows behind her. He wasn't speaking aloud – he was typing on his laptop. The computer was reading his words aloud and transmitting them directly to the girl's ear. But thanks to a program the boy had written that synthesized his vowel sounds and inflection patterns, it sounded almost exactly like his normal voice. Just as on-edge. Jumpy.

The girl hoped he was right about the transmitter. That it wouldn't interfere with the plane's navigation equipment, possibly causing a crash. And that it wouldn't be intercepted by any of the countless stations which monitored chatter from the skies. If that happened, they might be mistaken for terrorist hijackers. The plane could be shot down. They could die.

But he's never been wrong before, she thought.

"You've got six minutes max before the seat-belt sign is switched on," he said.

"And it'll take me less than four to do the job," the girl whispered. She didn't have to talk loudly for the boy to hear her. The speaker in her ear was connected to a needle so fine she'd barely felt it slip into the flesh behind her earlobe. The needle's point rested against her jawbone, detecting the minute vibrations created by her speech, and sending the sounds back to the boy's laptop.

"If he hasn't gone to the toilet yet, he's probably waiting for the landing," the boy said.

"Two more minutes. If he still hasn't moved in two minutes, we abort."

"Don't get caught."

"I never do," the girl replied.

The old woman in the window seat next to her snuffled in her sleep. The girl watched her for a moment. Not waking up, just dreaming. Bulbous eyes rolled under veiny lids. The girl turned her gaze back to the passenger in 8C, who was on the other side of the aisle a few rows in front of her. He was reading a newspaper, and showed no sign of getting up.

The girl glanced back down at her watch. One minute thirty before she would have to abort. She squeezed the arm of her seat, frustrated. There's a nineteen-carat alexandrite stone on this plane, she thought, worth at least $150,000. I know where it is, I know how to get to it, but I'm going to have to let it go because passenger 8C has a superhuman bladder.

Wait...

He was folding his newspaper. Raising the tray table. Unbuckling his seat belt.

"Okay," she whispered. "Operation High Heist is a go."

The girl pulled a magnet out of the seat pocket. It was an innocuous-looking thing – dull black, about the size of a matchbox. Ceramic, so it hadn't set off the metal detectors when she'd boarded the plane. She held it between her fingers, concealing it from anyone who might be watching.

The passenger walked past. The girl undid her seat belt and moved quickly and carefully up the aisle towards the empty seat. Most of the passengers were sleeping – the rest were absorbed in books and sudoku puzzles. No one looked up at her.

Each of her five senses was on high alert. She saw every flicker of movement, heard every tiny shuffle, felt every stray air current graze her skin. It was too much information to process consciously, so she let instinct take control. Her subconscious absorbed everything and pieced it together. Now, without looking, she knew the posture of each passenger, the shape and position of every bag, and the angle of vision from every sleepy eye.

She sat down in seat 8C – her movements unhurried but deliberate. There was a drawstring bag under the seat in front of her, some wrappers stuffed in the seat pocket, and the newspaper folded on the seat next to her. The paper was in French, which seemed unusual on a domestic flight.

But the girl wasn't interested in passenger 8C. He was incidental. She wanted the occupant of 9C, the seat behind her; a skinny middle-aged man with a magazine, a handlebar moustache and thick glasses that magnified his eyes. More specifically, she wanted the briefcase he had stowed under the seat at the beginning of the flight.

The seats between her and the window were empty. The occupants of the seats across the aisle appeared to be sleeping. Lucky.

She reached under her seat, and gently pulled the briefcase. As slowly and carefully as she could, she lifted it over the steel bar designed to stop luggage from sliding around during turbulence. Then she pulled it all the way out and put it on her lap.

"I've got the case," she breathed.

"Copy that," the boy said. "But hurry."

Until the turn of the century, briefcases containing valuables were handcuffed to the wrists of couriers. But there had been problems with this system. It was apparent to everyone who saw a case like this that it held expensive items, which is never good for security. Some thieves were good enough to pick the lock on the case while another held the attention of the courier. Others were brutal enough to hack off the courier's hand to release the cuffs.

Times had changed. These days, most briefcases used for transporting valuables had a proximity sensor in the lining. This sensor transmitted a signal once every tenth of a second to a watch the courier was wearing, and the watch bounced the signal back. If the briefcase and the watch were separated by two metres or more, the signal wouldn't make it. If half a second passed without the signal being received, alarms would sound at 110 decibels from both the briefcase and the watch.

The girl knew the watch couldn't be removed without a

five-digit numerical code. The briefcase couldn't be opened without the same code. The alarms couldn't be deactivated without opening the briefcase and removing the watch. Five digits – one hundred thousand possible combinations. And they were manual locks, not electronic. Impervious to electrical interference, and just as tough to crack by brute force.

The girl didn't have the code. The Source hadn't given it to her. So turning off the alarms was out. She had to crack open the briefcase and remove its contents without taking it more than two metres away from the courier's wrist. Then she had to put it back where she found it, and get back to her seat before passenger 8C came back from the toilet, or the courier noticed his briefcase was missing, or the captain switched on the seat-belt sign.

The lock had five scrolling wheels, currently set at 00000. The girl held the magnet above the first one and started turning it.

There was a thin iron block concealed under one digit in each of the wheels. If the blocks were face down in all five wheels, they created a bar, which slid aside so the case could be opened.

The iron block in the first wheel snagged the magnetic field and stopped it at 6. The girl moved on to the second wheel, which stopped at 5. The third wheel caught at 5 as well, and the fourth one rotated all the way to 9. The fifth one wouldn't turn at all, so the girl reasoned the block must be behind the zero.

Okay, she thought. 65590. Those are the digits that have to be face down.

She quickly worked out which digits would be on the opposite side of the wheels – those were the ones that had to be face up to make the correct combination. She just subtracted five from each one, with zero standing in for ten.

Easy – 10045 was the combination.

She took one last look around. The other passengers were still sleeping. The toilet light still said OCCUPIED. There was no indication that the courier had noticed that his briefcase was missing. Why should he, when the alarm on his wrist wasn't screaming?

The girl scrolled the dials around, lifted the latches on the sides of the case, and tried to raise the lid.

Snick. The lock slid across, the hinges swivelled, and the case opened up.

Her throat tightened with anticipation. Almost done, she thought.

The inside was padded with glittering grey foam. There was a bundle of tissue paper nestled in the centre.

The girl unfolded it as quickly as she dared. Then she put a hand to her mouth.

The object was made of alexandrite. But it wasn't just an uncut block, or even a geometrically sliced gem. It was a sculpture, chiselled to resemble the head of the ancient Greek god Hermes. The patron of thieves, if the girl recalled her ancient history class correctly. The stone sparkled with silent fireworks of green and red.

A block of uncut alexandrite would have been easy to sell. It could be passed off as a family heirloom or a mining acquisition, and sold to a jewellery workshop anywhere in the world. But this was so distinctive that it would be branded as stolen goods for ever. She and the boy didn't have the connections they would need to dispose of it cleanly.

The toilet light switched to VACANT, and the door shuddered as passenger 8C fumbled with it from the other side.

Hermes' curly hair sparkled as the girl folded the tissue paper around it and placed it in the foam. She closed the briefcase and scrolled all the dials back to zero.

"Operation aborted," she said.

PART ONE

Warning Signs

Ashley Arthur stood in front of the gleaming glass doors and gazed up at the HBS tower. It hadn't been difficult to find. Even if she hadn't spent an hour studying a map of the nearby roads, she would have seen it rising above the peaks of the surrounding buildings when she got off the bus. Although only twenty-five storeys high, the building was on a hilltop, with streets trickling down from all around it. And the Buckland logo, blooming from the roof of the tower, was a familiar part of the city's skyline; a giant yellow cubic sculpture with tapered edges and the company monogram in the top right corner. On sunny days it glittered in the sky; this afternoon it reflected the clouds in dull sepia. But still the building glowed, outshining the apartment building opposite and the KFC next door.

Today was a big day. Ash was pleased. Not exactly happy, or excited – but pleased. She'd worked long and hard to get here, and she was as close to achieving her goal as possible without actually having finished. She knew that was the most satisfying time of any project. Success wasn't hers just yet – but she could see it on the horizon. She could almost taste it.

Her phone rang – two short beeps. The noise sank into the ambience of the street without so much as a ripple, which was why she had picked that ringtone. Other people barely heard it.

Ash glanced at her watch: 4.12 p.m. She was ahead of schedule. She had time to take the call.

She read the caller ID. "Hi, Benjamin," she said.

"Hi, Double A," Benjamin said. "Nervous?"

"Have I ever been nervous before?"

"You've never met a billionaire before."

"I'll be fine," Ash said. She checked her reflection in the glass doors. Her oak-coloured hair was straight and tucked neatly behind her ears. Her jeans were clean, her blouse was crisp and white. She straightened the collar of her jacket. Her black wedges shone in the pasty daylight. She looked exactly how she should – like a fifteen-year-old with an important interview.

"Well, I'm here if you need me," Benjamin replied. He sounded a little jealous of her – up until now they'd been equal partners in the project. But today he'd feigned illness and taken the afternoon off school to be her remote support, so while she was meeting the richest man in the city, he would be sitting at home in front of his laptop, with his phone on the charger in case she needed him. He couldn't have come with her. He was observant, quick-thinking and skilled with technology, but he was nervous and awkward around strangers. Confidence was Ash's strength.

"You know me," Ash said. "I can handle this."

"I know. I'm not worried."

"You're always worried," Ash said. She'd never once seen Benjamin look relaxed. They'd first met the day after her sixth birthday – she had been sneaking into the school canteen after recess, hoping to plunder the leftover birthday cake before the teachers ate it with their lunch. During her search she'd found Benjamin hiding in the cupboard. Even as a five-year-old, he'd looked anxious. His fingers were twitching by his sides, and he was staring at Ash with suspicion. He had apparently formulated the same plan, only better – he had scoped out the location beforehand, located the cake on the bench by the sink, and stolen the *Oxford Dictionary of Quotations* from a classroom, intending to stand on it so he could reach.

The dictionary turned out not to be thick enough, so they stood it on its end and Benjamin held it steady while Ash tried to reach the cake. The plate was too heavy, and she dropped it. Fearing the noise would alert teachers, they both bolted, leaving behind a broken plate, a splattered cake and a ruined dictionary.

"What if he asks you questions about the essay?" Benjamin was saying.

"I've read it," Ash said. "No big deal."

A month ago, Narahm School for Girls, Ash's school, had announced a competition for the best economics essay. It would be judged by one of the richest businessmen in the country, and he would present a large cash prize to the winner in person. Ash told Benjamin about it, and he started writing.

They had won. Hammond Buckland had selected Benjamin's essay – "Taxes in a Globalized Nation", by Ashley Arthur – and now Ash was standing outside the headquarters of Hammond Buckland Solutions, while Benjamin sat in his bedroom in his empty house, wearing his pyjamas, coughing every time he answered the phone just in case it was his mother.

"If they try to take your phone away from you," Benjamin was saying, "let them. You can tell me what Buckland said later. But just in case they don't, I'll SMS you the new modem number in ten minutes. Call it when you can, then leave the call connected and I'll record the conversation onto my hard drive, okay?"

"We've been through this," Ash said. But she wasn't annoyed. Benjamin's obsessive reanalysis and repetition of their plans was what made him a good partner. He detected every flaw in any plan. "And by the way, you're a total geek."

"I know," Benjamin said. "Good luck, Double A."

"Don't need it," Ash said.

"In that case," Benjamin sounded hopeful now, "maybe I could take you out for a hot chocolate afterwards. To celebrate a job well done."

Ash watched a couple of women in charcoal suits stride out through the glass doors, talking animatedly. "You wish, Benjamin."

"You know, I really thought you'd say yes that time."

Ash smiled. Benjamin had been asking her out on dates regularly since they were twelve. She always turned him down, but he never seemed to mind.

"You didn't just hear me call you a geek?" she said. "Talk to you soon."

The doors slid aside as Ash stepped forward. Marble and glass loomed within. She took one last look up at the tip of the tower, at the gleaming cube high above. Then she walked inside.

There was an antechamber separating her from the main lobby, with a metal detector and an X-ray machine for bags. Cameras hummed from the corners of the ceiling. Three security guards, two men and a woman, looked at her incuriously.

Ash dumped her handbag on the conveyor belt and walked through the metal detector. It didn't beep. Her bag trundled out of the X-ray machine, and one of the guards started poking at it with what looked like a small vacuum cleaner. Sniffing for explosive residue, Ash knew. Checking that she wasn't going to bomb the place. She held her arms out sideways as the female security guard swept an identical device across her clothes.

"Thank you," one of the others said as he handed over her bag.

"No problem," Ash replied.

The main lobby was cleaner than most hospitals. Granite sparkled underfoot, wood panelling glowed under the reception counter, and mirrored glass walls reflected Ash's surprise back at her. She'd expected it to look classy, but for most office buildings classy just meant clean and sparse. This was more like walking into the reception area of a five-star hotel. It smelled of money.

The lifts were depositing a steady trickle of people into the lobby. They drifted past her towards the exit. Ash glanced at her watch – 4.20 p.m. Pretty soon everyone would be gone.

A receptionist with long, silver-painted nails looked up at her as she approached. "Hi," she said. "Can I help you?"

"My name's Ashley Arthur," Ash said. "I'm here to see Mr. Buckland."

The receptionist was already typing in her name by the time Ash had finished speaking. "The top floor, the twenty-fifth," she said, pointing into the alcove with the lifts. "You're a little early, so you might have to wait a while." She caught a name tag as a printer spat it out. "Wear this at all times. Security will hassle you otherwise."

"Sure," Ashley said, putting it around her neck. "Thanks."

The receptionist had already turned back to her computer.

Ash's wedges clacked against the granite. The many lift doors gleamed invitingly. She felt like everyone in the foyer was staring at her, like they could tell she didn't belong. She risked a glance. They weren't. Just nerves, she supposed. It was the most important day of her life, so she was entitled to be a little on edge. She pushed the button beside the lift, and watched the numbers scroll down on one of the indicators.

A woman with blood-red curls appeared beside her and pushed the down button. On her way to the basement car park, maybe. There was a ping, and the doors to a lift going up opened. Ash walked in and pushed the button for the twenty-fifth floor. It wasn't the top button; there was one for the roof as well. Ash wondered if someone went up to polish the yellow cube each day.

The doors slid shut. The interior of the lift looked like a miniature version of the lobby – granite floor, mirrored walls and wood panelling around the ceiling. It was so roomy Ash could have done a cartwheel.

As the lift began to ascend, the floor numbers blinked on a screen above her. At floor 6, the lift stopped. A guy with a silk suit and blue-framed glasses entered. He glanced at Ash's name tag but didn't speak to her. At floor 12, a man and two women joined them, muttering among themselves. Floor 13 brought a woman with a handbag designed to look like a slice of watermelon, and on floor 19 a man walked in who smelled faintly bitter, like old sweat, or a coin held in the hand for too long.

At floor 23 they all got out, and Ash travelled the last two floors alone. The lift was smooth and silent.

The doors slid open, and she stepped out of the lift.

A redwood-panelled corridor stretched away to either side. There were small paintings hanging on the walls, one every few metres along. Prints, not originals – there for the sake of atmosphere rather than art. Green mountains, vivid fruit bowls, faded lilies.

Ashley had studied a plan of the building, and knew that there were only conference rooms and bathrooms to her left. She turned right, and started walking.

She stared at her hands to check if they were shaking. They weren't. She was about to meet one of the world's wealthiest, smartest businesspeople. But she was still in absolute control.

A curly-haired man was sitting behind a marble counter up ahead. He looked up from his computer, and stood as she approached. "Hi," he said, sticking out his hand. "I'm Adam. Lovely to meet you, Miss Arthur."

He was in his mid-twenties, but was only a few centimetres taller than her. She thought she detected a trace of Welsh in his accent. His dark curls bobbed around a noble face. His sleeve slid up his outstretched arm, revealing that his watch-tan was slightly larger than his watch, like he'd bought a new one recently. His name tag read ADAM KEIGHLEY.

"Call me Ash," she said, shaking Keighley's hand. "Sorry I'm early."

"No problem. We have some very comfy chairs, and I

want to give you some background on Mr. Buckland and HBS before you go in anyway. Come with me."

Ash followed him down a corridor behind the counter. Looking back at the screen of the computer he'd been working on, she saw an open game of Minesweeper. Apparently it was there for the appearance of professionalism rather than for actual work. His work started now – talking to her.

"First time here?" Keighley asked.

Ash nodded.

"Lots of people have been before and don't realize it," Keighley said. "This building used to be a hotel. Mr. Buckland bought it, put the HBS cube on the roof, and now people forget it wasn't always our headquarters."

"Wouldn't it have been cheaper to buy an actual office building?" Ash asked.

"Offices usually rent out individual floors instead of selling the whole building. And Mr. Buckland wanted a certain image for the company: classy and unusual. Prestigious. This way, although employees are paid the same as they would be anywhere else, everyone wants a job here. We always hook the best applicants and, because our employees know their jobs are in high demand, they're more satisfied and they work harder."

"How many others are there?"

"Other what?"

"HBS buildings like this one."

Keighley smiled. "None. It's a global organization, but this is the only infrastructure."

"How long have you been working here?" Ash asked.

Keighley chuckled. "Is it that obvious?"

"That you're new?" Ash said. "Yeah. You still sound like a tour guide rather than an employee."

"Sorry. I've only been here a few weeks, and I studied hard for the job. Maybe too hard."

"No, it's fine." Ash stuck her hands in her pockets. "Give me the whole speech."

"Really?"

"Sure."

"Okay." Keighley clapped his hands together. "Hammond Buckland's first invention was the disposable wall. He knew that restaurants and schools were spending lots of money to fix the vandalism of their toilets, so he started selling thin sheets of clear plastic to stick to the exposed surfaces that could be removed at the end of the day or week."

Ash nodded. The toilet cubicles at her school were always shielded by them.

"The success of the disposable wall allowed Mr. Buckland to explore some other ideas. The collapsible subwoofer, the flash drive implant, the vacuum welcome mat. He hit the big time when he discovered a use for brewery protein – congealed protein that forms at the bottom of the vats during fermentation of beer. Every brewery in the world was just throwing it away, but Mr. Buckland reasoned that it must be either good for rats, or bad for rats, so if it was good he'd make food pellets, if it was bad he'd make rat poison."

"So which is it?"

Keighley grinned, showing small teeth. "Good, as it turns out. Rats can eat almost anything. Pet food is a good industry to be in, because the customer isn't the consumer, so the taste doesn't matter."

"Was that when he started AU?"

Keighley raised his eyebrows. "You've been studying too, I see."

Ash nodded. "I'm a customer, so I already know that bit of the speech." AU was a digital banking service which connected to an existing bank account, and added interest in exchange for use of the money while it was in the account. "Although I have one question."

Keighley nodded. "Go ahead."

"What does AU stand for?"

Keighley laughed. "It doesn't. It's the chemical symbol for gold."

Duh, thought Ash. I should have remembered that from school.

"Pretty soon Mr. Buckland decided to start a bricks-and-mortar bank," Keighley was saying. "HBS National. It cost more to run than AU, so it couldn't offer as high an interest rate, and a string of high-profile robberies of other banks forced us to increase security expenditure soon after it was formed. But it held out, and now flourishes in conjunction with AU."

Ash nodded. Her AU account was attached to her HBS National account, so she knew all about that too. But she hadn't wanted to interrupt Keighley again.

"And now Hammond Buckland Solutions is one of the world's biggest and most successful multinational corporations," Keighley concluded. "It has more than one million employees worldwide and an estimated worth of $4 billion."

"How much money does Mr. Buckland have?" Ash asked.

Keighley sighed. "Why did I know you were going to ask that?"

"You get that question a lot?"

"Kids always ask." He shrugged. "I don't know his net worth any more than he knows yours – it's private information. But *Business Review Weekly* estimated his personal fortune at $2.2 billion last year. Good enough?"

Ash smiled. "Excellent speech. Thank you."

"And here we are."

They were facing two large doors, panelled with what looked like oak. The handles were gold plated, but the doors didn't look glamorous – they had a sparse, vault-like simplicity.

There were two security guards, one on either side of the door. Their uniforms were a sharp grey, with a yellow square on the right shoulder of each – the HBS logo. Their faces were as expressionless as those of the Buckingham Palace guards.

Keighley glanced at his watch. "We've still got a couple of minutes to spare," he said. "Take a seat."

Ash sank into one of the giant black couches lining the walls. A clock on the wall read 4.28 p.m. Keighley sat behind a desk, identical to the one she'd seen him at before. He turned to the computer and brought up a half-finished game of Minesweeper – Ash wondered if it was the same game he'd been playing on the other screen.

She slipped her phone out of her pocket and hit SEND. The phone silently dialled Benjamin's modem, and connected. She switched the keypad to LOCK and pocketed the phone. Now Benjamin would be able to hear everything Hammond Buckland said when she was in his office.

The phone on Keighley's desk rang; two beeps and a chirp. Keighley poked it.

"Send Miss Arthur in," the speakerphone said. The voice

was flat and distracted. Arthur recognized it from an interview she'd watched on TV – it was Buckland.

Keighley minimized Minesweeper and tapped out a combination on the keyboard. The huge doors emitted a muffled clank.

Keighley nodded to her. "Whenever you're ready."

Ash stood up, and smoothed her blouse down at the front. She tilted her head from side to side, cracking her neck, like a tennis player preparing to serve. She walked to the doors, took a deep breath, and pushed.

The Interview

I hate government jobs, Michael Peachey thought.

He was waiting outside HBS in the white Ford sedan that had been provided for him. Through the tinted windows he watched pedestrians bustling back and forth, other drivers drumming their fingers on their steering wheels. A window washer finished wiping the first pane of the top floor, lowered his platform a level, and started on the one below. The HBS logo shone high above, a surrogate sun for the overcast day.

He checked his pocket watch. Ten past four. Damn government, he thought.

When a gang hired him, a tattooed thug would give him a cash advance in a darkened back alley. That was fine. When it was a corporation, he would usually get a call on a secure line, or an encrypted email. That was okay. But when the government wanted his services, it got so complicated. They demanded disguises, intermediaries, false names, code words, foreign accounts. They wanted control over everything.

They had forbidden Peachey to enter the building before 4.15.

Peachey was wearing a dark grey suit. Not expensive, not cheap. His hair was cropped short, and had a touch of wax. His five o'clock shadow was only visible close up. His tinted glasses were small. He looked average in every way. Anyone who noticed him would forget him before he left their field of vision.

He was supposed to wait for the girl to arrive before going in. She was Buckland's last official appointment of the day, so if she didn't turn up, Buckland might actually leave his office before Peachey could reach him. He had told the government agent that this wouldn't be an issue. He was good at improvising. But she had insisted. "We will accept no departure from the plan," she said. "Deviation will incur penalties."

When Peachey had met the agent, he wasn't supposed to know who she was. But he did. Her white gold watch had the letters TW engraved on the face. There were nineteen government employees in this state with those initials. Only eight of those were women, only three of those were high up enough to be assigned to him, and only one of those had Korean ancestry.

All of this was on the public record. Thanks to the Freedom of Information Act, the government wasn't allowed to conceal the identities of its employees. Peachey could have walked right in to the federal police building and asked for a list.

Her name was Tania Walker, and until recently she'd been an operative for Terrorism Risk Assessment. She'd left active duty in TRA to become a "consultant". Peachey knew what that meant. She was in charge of off-the-books jobs, operations that the government couldn't afford to be linked to.

Jobs like this one.

Peachey had watched the girl talk on her phone for more than five minutes before going in. This was already a deviation from the plan. She was supposed to walk right in and keep Buckland there.

Maybe she would get caught in the crossfire later. He smiled at the thought.

When the glass doors slid shut behind her, Peachey climbed out of the Futura. For once, he didn't bother wiping his fingerprints off the interior surfaces. One of the benefits of working for the government, he thought, is that they short-circuit any investigation afterwards. Sometimes they even find a scapegoat. They protect you from the police. They have to, in order to protect themselves.

He strolled in through the glass doors. Like he worked there. Like he *belonged* there. That was his gift. He could blend in anywhere.

He had no bag to put through the X-ray machine. The metal detector didn't pick up the gun in the holster under his arm. It was a Glock 7, German made, high-density ceramic rather than metal. Expensive and undetectable. The explosive residue sniffer didn't pick it up either – it had never been fired. The holster was a complex tangle of leather and plastic, customized to the gun and his ribs so there was no visible bulge under his suit. Good for a quick draw, too, although the straps made reholstering it a little clumsy.

When he was inside the lobby, the silver-nailed receptionist greeted him and accepted his cover story with a minimum of fuss. Yes, Mr. Buckland was expecting him. Yes, he could go straight on up. Peachey kept his hands mobile: smoothing his lapels, silently clicking his fingers, roaming slowly across the desk. This was a habit of his, designed to draw her gaze away from his face. The receptionist printed out his name tag and told him that Buckland's office was on the twenty-fifth floor. He thanked her and headed for the lifts.

My name is Michael Peachey, he narrated in his head. I'm a hit man.

Peachey stepped into the lift and pushed the button. Keeping his head low and his arms by his sides, he gave the mirror his best sociopathic stare. Lips slightly parted, showing teeth. Head bowed, eyes steely.

Perfect. Exactly how an assassin should look. Peachey continued talking to his imaginary audience as the doors slid closed.

I put the same three shots into every victim. Torso left, torso right, head. In the decade I've been doing that, I've never missed. There's an index of the world's top fifty assassins, judged on experience, success rate and skill with their chosen weapon. Known as The List, it's on a server in a basement in Beijing, but you can access it from anywhere in the world if you have the contacts, the money and a password. Last time I checked, I was number three. Number two was Jeremy Quay, number one was Alex de Totth – and I happen to know that Quay is dead.

Someday Peachey planned to write an autobiography. He had enough money to buy a new identity and vanish – it wouldn't be hard, given that few people knew his name and even fewer knew his face. He'd move to another country, and send the book to a publisher. They'd print it, because it would be well-researched, his writing rich with details. Plus he wouldn't ask for royalties. How could he, without compromising his new identity? But then someone would buy the film rights, and he'd show up at the audition. Just a no-name actor from somewhere in South America. And he'd get the part, because who could play Michael Peachey better than Michael Peachey?

This dream was unlikely to come true, of course. Most days it all just felt like idle fantasy. But today it seemed close. He had a good feeling about this job.

I know Quay's dead because I killed him, he recited. It wasn't out of rivalry – it was just business. Someone hired him to kill a very rich woman. She found out, hired me, and I killed Quay before he could get to her.

Shame. He was a nice guy, for a contract killer.

As for de Totth, well, she took a big job about six months ago. No word from her since, and I figure the government tried to hire her to kill Buckland before contacting me. They have access to The List, and they can afford the best.

This is a risky business. You don't hear from someone in six months, chances are you're never going to again. Given that the government didn't hire her for this job, I suspect I'm now the number one.

Peachey hummed along with the soundtrack to this part of his imagined movie – a crunching, echoing beat, and a growling synth to build up tension.

A few other people entered the lift on the eighth floor. A young man, chatting on his mobile phone. A dark-suited woman, tapping immaculate nails against the wall. A middle-aged guy wearing huge glasses.

The numbers on the screen scrolled up. The biggest set represented the floor this lift was on, but there were smaller numbers on either side, telling him which floors the other lifts were on. He wondered why anyone would need to know.

The doors slid open, and he stepped out onto Buckland's floor. There was a curly-haired guy sitting behind another reception desk.

"Hi," the guy said. "I'm Adam. A pleasure to meet you, Mr. Ford."

"Call me Joseph," Peachey said. "I'm here to negotiate the sale of Syndicate Studios. Is Mr. Buckland—"

"Yes, your secretary called ahead," the receptionist said. "Mr. Buckland is looking forward to meeting with you to discuss the matter. He's otherwise engaged just now, but has you booked in for five o'clock. So if you'd like to follow me..."

Just like Walker said it would be, Peachey thought. He followed the receptionist down a wood-panelled corridor speckled with obnoxiously bright paintings. It smelled of carpet cleaner. They passed an emergency stairwell, a few conference rooms and a bathroom. Peachey took particular notice of the stairwell. This was a long corridor – after killing Buckland he probably wouldn't want to run all the way to the other end and wait for a lift. Taking the fire stairs seemed like a much better idea, particularly as they should be deserted.

He grinned. Actually, maybe he should set off the fire alarm, making the stairs horribly crowded. He could blend in, disappear, and have a coffee across the road as he watched the HBS employees line up outside, pleasantly surprised by the forced early finish. He'd taken to staying nearby for a coffee after his assignments were complete, partly because he was a caffeine addict, but mostly because the coffee shop next door was the last place the police ever searched for a murderer.

"Been working here long?" Peachey asked. Mundane conversation might distract the receptionist enough to leave no lasting memory of his appearance.

"Why does everyone ask me that?"

"You're cheerful. Corporate life hasn't crushed your spirit."

The receptionist laughed. Peachey read his name tag: KEIGHLEY.

"Well, give it time," Keighley said. "But I have to say, it's been fairly easy so far. Main reception downstairs finds out who's who, security up here deals with anyone who doesn't do what they're told. Nothing left for me to do but show up on time, look respectable, and lead people from one end of this corridor to the other." He grinned. "And, of course, act cheerful. Here we are."

Peachey stared past the two security guards to the huge oak doors. They more or less ruled out killing Keighley and the guards before being admitted. He'd never be able to break them down, and he lacked the tools to pick the lock. He'd have to preserve his cover for a little longer.

Keighley went behind his desk and pulled what looked like a price-tag scanner out from under his desk, and tapped a few keys on the computer. He approached Peachey. "Hold still for a second."

Peachey tried to look relaxed as Keighley reached towards him with the scanner and pointed it at the name tag. He didn't like being this close to people who weren't clients or targets. But he told himself that Keighley was staring at the name tag, not his face – and that he'd probably have to kill him on the way out anyhow.

The gun made a faint hiss, and Keighley took it away.

"What was that about?" Peachey asked.

"I just activated the barcode in your tag. If security ever approaches you, just hold out the tag so they can scan it. The tag tells them your name, your business here, and which floor you're not allowed above, and the barcode proves it's legit." Keighley smiled. "The floor numbers are the same as the security levels, and you're allowed to be on any floor up to your level. You're a temporary level 25, obviously."

Peachey doubted this would be useful to him; in a few minutes he planned to be well past handing his tag to guards to scan. But he smiled. "So I'm not allowed to go to the roof, then?"

"Not a lot to see up there," Keighley said. "A big cube, and about a million cigarette butts. Take a seat." He glanced at his wristwatch. "Mr. Buckland will see you in a few minutes."

Peachey removed his pocket watch from his breast pocket. He'd never been able to own wristwatches, because he had thick wrists and very narrow hands. Watches fell right off, unless he tightened them so much that he lost circulation. The pocket watch was annoyingly distinctive, but he told himself that his appearance was so bland that witnesses would remember the watch rather than him.

He settled in to wait.

Buckland's office was less like an office than the foyer of a resort. Chilled daylight poured through wall-sized double-glazed windows. A few convincing ferns stroked the air by the air vents. An apparently original Giger hung on the wall, a carefully measured stain of darkness amongst the polished hardwood panels – a marked contrast to the cheery prints outside. There were shelves of bottles and glasses and a bench with a sink. Maybe Buckland invited people here for parties as well as meetings. An empty scuba suit stood in the corner. Ashley's eyes widened as she turned – there was a large spa to the side, with cornflower-blue water lapping at the pale tiles around the edge.

Despite this, the room had a lived-in feeling. A long overcoat hung from a hook behind the door. A briefcase leaned against the wall. There was a dish on a side table with a wallet and keys sitting in it.

"I spend as much time here as at home," Buckland said from behind his desk. "Why confine my luxuries to night-time?" He stood up and offered his hand. "Good to meet you, Miss Arthur."

"Call me Ash," she said as she approached. She'd seen him on TV a few times over the past three or four years, on a couple of magazine covers, and on ads for his various companies and products. He looked smaller in real life, the way most famous people do. Something about their epic fortunes, Ash thought, their massive influence, their huge reputations and tremendous houses make you feel like they should tower over you, like you should be in their shadow. But when you meet them in the flesh, they're people-sized. Buckland's outstretched, latte-coloured fingers were only a little longer than hers. His golden-brown eyes were level with hers, and he was only stooping a little.

"Congratulations on an exquisite essay," Buckland said.

Ash grinned. "Thank you, sir."

"I didn't expect to read an entry that matched my own thoughts on the issues so precisely. Was that your aim, or just a fluke?" He sat down again. "You've already won, so you can be honest."

"Coincidence, sir," Ash said. "I'd been researching the issue before the competition was announced, so I thought I'd go with my strengths."

Buckland looked sceptical. "You were researching tax law problems for global corporations recreationally?"

"I plan for them to be my problems someday, sir."

"Interesting. Is that because you want to own a corporation, or because you want to be a tax lawyer?" He gestured at the chair opposite his desk. "Take a seat. And there's no need to call me sir."

"Thanks, Mr. Buckland." Ash sat down. The city sprawled out in front of her, uncaring and powerful, looming behind the windows like a shark in a tank.

"I'll tell you a secret," Buckland said. He leaned forward. "You don't want to own a major corporation. Trust me."

Ash stared at him. "That seems a strange thing for you to say."

"Who'd know better than me?"

"You didn't get this far by accident."

"No, you're right." Buckland turned his chair sideways, and gazed out at the city. "I didn't."

There was a pause. "So you built your empire," Ash said, "and now you don't want it any more?" She smiled. "Can I have it?"

Buckland laughed. "That's what I'm saying. You don't want it."

Ash wasn't sure what she'd expected from this conversation. But this wasn't it. When she was a child, her mother had told her that money was the most important thing in the world, because it could be traded for almost anything. Money bought success, and respect, and happiness. Ash hadn't imagined that a billionaire like Hammond Buckland would disagree.

"Statistics dictate that I will live for roughly another forty years," Buckland was saying. "Divide $2.2 billion by forty, and you know what you get?"

Ashley frowned and thought for a minute. "Roughly $55 million?"

Hammond Buckland raised his eyebrows. "Exactly $55 million. Your maths is as good as your writing."

"Just a lucky guess, Mr. Buckland," she said. Maybe Benjamin was starting to rub off on her.

"Well anyway, my living expenses are nowhere near

$55 million per year. Like most people, I'd settle for a nice home, a big TV, a holiday once a year, and a car that always starts. That would cost only a fraction of my savings. In fact, I'm currently earning money at a much faster rate than I could possibly spend it. I'm forced to save."

"Lots of people would kill to have that problem," Ash said.

"You'd be surprised how small a consolation that is. What's the point in having money you can't use? I spent my whole life lusting after wealth, and I didn't think about what I'd do when I had it until it was too late."

"But why is that such a problem?"

Buckland sighed. "Because I can't buy back the things I had before I was rich. Anonymity, for instance. My face isn't that famous, but I can't sign a cheque without being stared at, or called a liar or both. And companionship – I can't make friends, or go on dates. Anyone I get close to will either be trying to exploit me, or they'll be at risk of being abducted."

"Have you thought about giving the money away?" Ash asked.

"To a stranger on the street?" Buckland shrugged. "Their bank would never be able to cash the cheque. Unless they were with my bank, and I don't even know what would happen there. It'd be like a snake eating its own tail. And I can't sell the company, either – no one can afford to buy it for what it's worth, and if I try to sell it for less, the stock market will collapse."

"I meant to charities," Ash said. "Becoming a philanthropist."

"I've tried that. It's hard to find charities that won't spend it on advertising or converting people to their own cause. And even with the good ones, it turns out there's only so much they can use. If you give a charity with too few resources too much money, they drown in it. The imbalance makes them collapse. It ends up being way more effective for me to build my own homeless shelters, send food to Africa myself, buy my own sections of rainforest for conservation. And I've been doing all these things, but my fortune keeps growing. I'm not spending enough. And the government tries to stop me."

"The government?" Ash and Benjamin had researched the influence of governments on the rich and vice versa for the essay, and hadn't come across anything to suggest that wealthy individuals were discouraged from donating to charities. "Why?"

"Because I have no family or friends," Buckland said. "And as such, I have no legal will. If I die, the running of the company goes to the various people below me on the ladder. But my majority holding of shares in HBS, my personal possessions and all of my savings will go to the government.

So they want me to stay as rich as possible, so someday they can have it all."

Ash's eyes widened. "Doesn't the government have way more money than you anyway?"

"Our nation is wealthy, but not so wealthy that my fortune is negligible to the economy. Particularly with our foreign debt, and the war costing us billions."

"And they've tried to stop you from donating to charity?"

"They try to stop me spending any money on anything," Buckland said. "Particularly anything overseas. They don't like my money leaving the country. At first they arranged special discounts for me on local products, equipment, labour, whatever. When they realized I didn't care, they started putting huge tariffs on foreign things so that it's impractical for me to have any connection to any kind of business outside our country."

"Are they allowed to do that?"

"They never do it directly. From time to time I get singled out by another big company as someone you shouldn't trade with, and I can see the government pulling the strings above. When they can't do that, they change the law so it stops everyone from doing what I was trying to do. That way I can't claim bias."

"But no one else notices because no one else is rich enough to be able to do those things anyway?" Ash tried to keep the cynicism out of her voice.

"Exactly," Buckland said. "So here's my advice: don't get greedy. Think about your goals before you make them. And when you reach the finish line, don't just keep running out of habit. Take a moment to rest, be proud of what you've accomplished, think about how lucky you are. Otherwise you'll wake up someday and realize you're working yourself to death for a life you never really wanted."

Ashley rested her hands on his desk. "So what are you going to do?"

"Me?" Buckland smiled. "I'm leaving the country. Tomorrow. I'm changing my name and going to a place where no one reads *Business Review Weekly*."

The scuba suit made more sense now – although Ash wondered why he had it out already. "Really? I hadn't heard that."

"Of course not. It's a secret."

"Won't the government try to stop you?" Ashley stared at him. "Doesn't that kind of interfere with their plans for your money?"

"Let them try," Buckland said. "But there's nothing they can do."

Why is he telling me this? Ash thought. He doesn't know anything about me.

"Anyway, here's your cheque," Buckland said. He handed

Ash an envelope. "Ten thousand dollars; congratulations. Any plans for spending it?"

"Nope. I'm putting it in my AU account," Ash said. "I'll have earned $350 interest by the end of the year."

Buckland frowned. "You mean $700, don't you?"

Ash winced inwardly. She was splitting the prize money with Benjamin, but Buckland wasn't supposed to know that.

"Yes," she said, "of course. Sorry, I'm just excited."

"And here," Buckland said, rummaging through his desk, "is a voucher entitling you to two regular coffees. You can either use it at the café downstairs, or at any coffee shop on this street – I own them all."

He handed her a card in a little plastic wallet. "I know I've just given you enough money for about three thousand reasonably priced coffees, but the cheque will take a couple of days to clear, and I figured you might want one to celebrate right away."

Ashley laughed. "Thanks, Mr. Buckland."

"You're welcome," he said. He glanced at his watch. "This has been fun, but I'm supposed to be meeting a potential business partner at five o'clock. No rest for the wicked." He offered his hand. "Nice to meet you."

"You too," Ash said, shaking it. "Good luck with your travels."

"Thanks. And please don't tell anyone about that until I'm gone. You wouldn't want to spoil the surprise, right?"

Ash shook her head. "I'll keep my mouth shut. Least I can do."

"Excellent." Buckland punched in a combination on his keyboard, and Ash heard the locks on the big doors click open. "Well, goodbye."

Ash turned to look at him once more as she approached the doors. He was already engrossed in other things, removing a piece of paper from his desk drawers with one hand and typing with the other. They would probably never meet again – the next time she saw him might be on the news, as the media realized he'd skipped town.

She twisted the handle and walked through.

Keighley smiled at her. "Hello again." He nodded at a man sitting on the couch, in the same spot Ash had occupied while she was waiting. "Mr. Ford? You can go in now."

The man looked up from his pocket watch, stood, and straightened his suit. He barely looked at Ashley as he walked past her through the doors. They swung shut behind him.

"Well, how was that?" Keighley asked. "Exciting?"

· "Yeah, it was great."

"Can I take you to the cafeteria, or are you going straight home?"

Ash needed to discuss the conversation with Benjamin.

"It's okay, I'll show myself out. I need to use the bathroom first. Is there one on this floor?"

Keighley pointed down the corridor they had arrived through. "Third on the right. There's another lift you can use there. Remember to hand in your name badge on your way out."

"Thanks." Ashley started walking. When she was out of sight and earshot around the corner, she put her phone to her ear. "Still there?"

"How weird was that?" Benjamin said. "I didn't expect a 'money is the root of all evil' lecture."

"Neither did I. But you see our new problem?"

"He's leaving the country tomorrow."

"That's right," Ash said. "Someone else will take over, and the first thing they'll do is demand an inventory of the building."

"So either he'll take the loot with him, or they'll find it."

"Exactly. So now we have a time limit. Wherever he's hidden the money, we have to find it and get it out today. Before the building closes. This is our last chance."

"I don't know about this," Benjamin said. "You think we can still do it?"

Ash bit her lip. She knew that professional thieves usually got busted because they got too confident, too spontaneous, too greedy. They tried to take more than they could carry. She and Benjamin had never done a job this big. They'd never worked without a solid plan. They were breaking all the rules. They should abort.

But it was *so much money*.

"We can do it," she said.

Peachey was reaching for his Glock even as the doors swung shut behind him. When my life is made into a movie, he thought, this part of the soundtrack will be heavy metal. Guttural guitars and bass-rich drums, more felt than heard. But with an electronic touch – Rammstein, maybe, or Marilyn Manson.

In the split second it took him to raise his weapon he was taking a mental snapshot of the room. The first quality of a good hit man was the ability to leave everything exactly as it was found. Spa. Desk. Scuba suit. Pot plant. Painting. Chairs.

Empty.

Peachey swung around. The office was empty. There was no sign of Buckland.

Peachey ducked into a crouch. Partly because he wanted to check under the tables and chairs, partly because in his line of work it was strategically good to duck whenever something didn't seem right. A crosshair could be pointed at the back of your skull.

Buckland wasn't under the furniture. Peachey looked up.

He wasn't clinging to the roof, either.

Peachey scoured the room with increasing fury. No hidden doors in the walls, floor or ceiling. The windows weren't the kind that opened, and it was a twenty-five-storey drop anyhow. He'd been watching the door the whole time, so he knew that Buckland hadn't escaped that way.

Had he ever been in here in the first place?

"I've been expecting you..."

Peachey whirled back around towards the desk. He could see no one.

"...Mr. Peachey."

Peachey turned the computer monitor around. Hammond Buckland's face stared grimly out of it.

"I know why you're here," Buckland continued. "I know who sent you. I know your success rate is good – excellent, even – but I also know that today will be an exception."

Peachey turned away from the monitor, put down the Glock, and tried to push the desk to one side. Maybe there was a trapdoor under it. But it was heavy, and barely budged. He picked up the gun.

"You've met your match. You're at my mercy. Just count yourself lucky that I have nothing to gain from killing you, and plenty to lose by giving you to the cops."

Peachey wrenched the black painting off the wall. There was only wood behind it.

"I assure you that finding me is the least of your concerns," Buckland warned. "You may have noticed that the doors are now locked. You probably didn't notice the room slowly filling with a colourless, odourless gas."

Peachey stared at the monitor, heart pounding.

"It's an airborne barbiturate. Non-lethal, but I'd say you have about..." Buckland glanced down off camera, probably at his watch, "...two minutes before you lose consciousness."

Peachey couldn't smell any change in the air, but he could hear a faint hissing. He closed his eyes. It was coming from the corner of the room.

Opening his eyes, he saw that the fern closest to the window had a plastic nozzle among its green fingers. His vision sparkled as he neared it, and he gasped. He stumbled back towards the desk.

"You have three options," Buckland said. "One: wait for the gas to knock you out. You'll be taken from the room, locked up in a holding cell in the basement, then I'll use you as a bargaining chip against the government. Two: call for backup. Your employers might send someone for you, and that person might arrive in time, and they might be instructed to rescue you instead of executing you. But I wouldn't count on it."

Peachey exhaled, expelling the gas from his lungs. He clamped his jaw shut and pinched his nose. He'd never held his breath longer than three minutes, and he could already feel the sedative in the gas spilling through his brain.

"Your third option is to throw your gun into the spa. There's a pair of handcuffs on my desk; put them on. If you do exactly as I say, the doors will unlock themselves, the gas will be fanned out, and you'll be escorted from the building. Then you'll be free to go."

Peachey kicked the monitor off the desk. The LCD cracked, and Buckland's face vanished. The speakers kept talking: "No hurry. You have until you lose consciousness to decide. One minute and thirty seconds."

Peachey gritted his teeth. He didn't negotiate with his targets. He never surrendered. Buckland would pay for this.

He ran to the door, his lungs already aching. He leaped into the air, right foot first, and tried to break it down.

Thud. It was like kicking concrete. The wood didn't give at all. Peachey fired his Glock into the panelling. The shot sounded like a shovel hitting granite, and Peachey saw steel in the bullet holes. The door was wood-panelled metal. Impossible to get through.

Peachey fired five more shots, *blamblamblam! blamblam!* One into each of the walls, one into the floor, and one into the ceiling. He got the same reaction from each surface. Buckland's office was a steel tomb.

His head was becoming light. He tried to focus. It was obvious that he was never going to find the hidden passageway in time. So what were his other options? Think!

Then he saw something. Something that could get him out of this.

Peachey pointed his Glock at the double-glazed windows and pulled the trigger.

The glass disintegrated, shards curling outward into the daylight like the teeth of an eel as it opens its jaws. The wind outside blasted Peachey's hair back, roaring in his ears, but he could still hear the hissing of the pot plant. The gas was coming into the room faster now. Peachey dropped the gun; he hated leaving it behind, but one hand was covering his nose, he needed the other one free, and he didn't have time to reholster it.

He ran towards the window, and threw himself into the void.

The two steel cables he'd seen were about two metres apart. Peachey reached for the left one and grabbed it with one hand, still unwilling to uncover his nose with the other. He squinted against the wind, which pushed up from the alley far, far below. The cable burned his palm as he slid down it.

Bang! The window washer whirled around in alarm as Peachey crashed down onto his platform. Peachey grabbed the platform for support as it wobbled crazily underneath him. He gulped air desperately, and it flowed swiftly into his lungs, cold and sweet.

"What the hell are you doing?" the window washer screamed. "Are you crazy?"

Peachey grabbed the top of the man's head with his free hand and twisted. With a muffled *crick*, he broke the window washer's neck. Peachey squeezed each of the buckles on the man's harness, popping them loose. Then he looked down, took aim, and pushed the body over the side.

A few seconds later, the window washer landed in the alleyway dumpster between HBS and the KFC. The faint crash leaked back up through the air to Peachey. Good thing the lid was open, he thought. It's tall enough that no one will see in without standing on tiptoes. The cleaner should be buried in batter crumbs during the dinner rush. Peachey turned to the window the platform was facing.

I could lower this down to the ground, he thought as he buckled himself into the washer's harness, and walk away. Skip town, and hope the government doesn't come looking for me. That would be the smart thing to do.

But he wouldn't do it. Buckland had tricked him. Peachey was lucky not to be arrested or dead. And that infuriated him.

Peachey started winching the platform back up to the roof. He would find Buckland, and he would kill him. In his last moments of life, Buckland would realize that he'd been defeated, and he would wish he'd never messed with Michael Peachey.

"Met my match, huh?" Peachey grunted as he twisted the winch. "We'll see about that."

Treasure Hunt

The Hammond Buckland Operation had started when Ashley and Benjamin were planning a robbery at an HBS National in another city. Their first draft of the plan involved Ash drilling into the bank's vault from above, where the walls were thinnest and where the cameras weren't pointing. They knew how to cut the power to the cameras and the rest of the grid simultaneously when she got inside so that it wouldn't look like sabotage. And they knew that the money in the vault was only counted once every two days, so provided they only took a few bricks of cash, they'd be back in their hometown before anyone even realized there had been a robbery. Their problem was working out how to cover the noise of the drilling. Ash had suggested placing a few layers of insulation on the roof and drilling through them. Benjamin had suggested waiting for a thunderstorm.

They forgot all about the bank when they received a new tip-off from the Source.

Ash and Benjamin had been career thieves for eighteen months now. Their plans had become more elaborate and diabolical as their procurements had gotten bigger and more valuable. They moved up from the surgical art of safe-cracking to intricately choreographed thefts of luxury cars, from daylight robberies of small mansions to moonlit incursions into posh art galleries. They never went for the easy targets. They liked a challenge.

The point wasn't just acquiring material things. It was identifying the impossible, and doing it.

The first thing they told Ash when she started at Narahm School for Girls was that each student had limitless potential. They could run for office. They could be famous artists. They could compete at the Olympics, or win the Nobel Peace Prize. There was nothing they couldn't do.

The next thing they told her was to always wear the school blazer, and keep her socks pulled up. To never leave the premises during school hours. To walk, not run, through the school corridors. To only work on her personal projects after all her homework was done.

They gave her all that potential, and then they took it all away.

Ash could pick a Lockwood padlock in under twenty seconds. She could scale a chain-link fence with less than 8 decibels of noise. She could hit a 10-centimetre bullseye from 20 metres with a dart from a blowpipe. She could rewire any back-to-base alarm system so it went off as she was leaving, rather than arriving – and therefore wouldn't be replaced when the robbery was discovered.

This was the appeal of her work. Knowing that she was using her full potential, and that she was really good at what she did.

They had first started stealing because Ash had needed the money. Her mother was a divorce lawyer, and had managed to take most of the family's money with her when she left Ash's father. She'd twisted the law so that she wasn't required to pay child support either, and Ash's dad was barely making enough to keep the phone connected. Ash had decided it was better to steal to support herself than watch her dad go bankrupt trying to keep her comfortable.

Benjamin had first started because Ash was his best friend. He would follow her anywhere, do anything for her, and if she was going to be a thief, he was going to be one too.

The Source had first contacted them through Benjamin's gmail account. He or she sent a list of the locations and dates of all the jobs Ash and Benjamin had done in the past six months. And at the bottom, there was one location they'd never been to, with a date that wouldn't arrive for three days. After that there was one word – "*Interested?*" – with a link to a secure server.

They had panicked. No way were they clicking the link – the police were obviously on to them, and were trying to lure them into a trap. What should they do? How could they save themselves?

But four days later, they saw a story on the news about federal agents finding $700,000 in a storage unit. Apparently the drug lord who rented it had died of a heart attack months ago, leaving his lease to expire.

The storage unit was the location in the Source's email.

The Source sent them a few more emails. Each had a location, a date and a link. At first, Ash and Benjamin were still suspicious – even if it wasn't the police, someone was playing games with them. Who, and why? So they started clicking the links, in order to investigate. Behind each one, they found a description of something valuable. Something that would be in a specific place, at a specific time, briefly exposed. Vulnerable. And there was always a bank account number, to deposit 15 per cent of the profits after the job – the informer's cut.

They didn't know how the Source had found them. But they knew he or she was offering them a fortune. And it wasn't long before they received an email about Hammond Buckland.

The place? HBS. The prize? *Two hundred million dollars*.

The link led them to a document that detailed Buckland's financial history, including all his exploits, corporations, profits and expenses. The information was mostly on the public record, but there were a few things, like account balances from Buckland's bank statements, that must have been stolen. And the Source had highlighted one spot where the numbers didn't add up. At exactly the time Buckland purchased what was now the HBS building and started refurbishing it, $200 million mysteriously disappeared. There were no other expenditures. No acquisitions. No other infrastructure. There was only one place the money could be.

Benjamin and Ash were excited. There was a fortune hidden somewhere in the HBS building, and only they knew it was there. So they started planning.

Benjamin went into HBS one day, with a cover story about an economics project. It didn't get him beyond the lobby, but he was able to take a few snapshots of the vacuum bots – the squat, circular robots that rolled quietly around each floor, sucking dust out of the carpet and polishing the floor tiles. Having established the make and model, he ordered one on eBay. When it arrived, he took it to pieces and planted a tiny camera next to the motion sensor and a transmitter behind the wheels. Then he repackaged it, went back into HBS, and poured a cup of coffee into the motion sensor of one of theirs. Without a working sensor, the bot started bumping into walls and people. Benjamin went back home, and waited.

It took three days for HBS to notice the fault. It took two days for them to establish it couldn't be fixed and order a new one. It took one day for the company that made the robots to send a delivery driver with a replacement. And it took twenty-two seconds for Ash to steal the robot out of the truck, leaving Benjamin's modified version in its place.

Ash hadn't asked why they didn't just switch one of the robots at HBS for theirs. Benjamin told her anyway.

"Firstly because the robots map out each floor as they move so they can clean with the most efficient route," he said. "Our one wouldn't know the floor plan, because it was new. This would cause the engineers at HBS to believe it was faulty and open it up, then they might spot our camera and transmitter. And secondly, because HBS puts chips in everything they own, so it sets off the alarms any time someone tries to take it outside the building. It had to be a new one."

"We could have thrown the old robot in the garbage inside the building," Ash said.

"Then the alarms would go off when they emptied the bins. They'd find the robot, and wonder why they had one too many." Benjamin winked at her. "But you're thinking. I like that."

"Don't patronize me," Ash said.

It took a few days for the robot to be used on all of the 25 floors. Once it was done, Benjamin and Ash watched about five hours of footage in total. They watched it do a full lap of every floor. They didn't see anything that looked like it might be worth $200 million.

"That was like a *Lord of the Rings* marathon," Ash said. "I can't believe we watched all that for nothing. Could the money be on a high shelf, where the robot can't see?"

Benjamin was smiling. "I doubt it."

"What are you grinning about? Do you know where it is?"

"No. But we know where it's not."

Benjamin instructed the transmitter to send the robot's absorbed map to them. A few seconds later, his screen filled up with files – a floor plan for each of the 25 floors. He opened them, one at a time.

Ash was starting to understand. She rubbed her hands together in anticipation. "There are places it doesn't go," she guessed.

"Yep. Four of them." Benjamin sat back in his chair. "Buckland's office, on the 25th floor. The car park in the basement. And two rooms on the 24th floor, one in the north corner, one in the south. One of those rooms will make us rich. So how do we get inside to check them out?"

They came up with several plans, including applying for internships, pretending their parents worked there, breaking in just before dawn, when security was lightest and escaping would be easiest. But they needn't have bothered. Less than a month later the essay competition was announced. A month after that, they'd won. And two weeks later, Ash was standing in the corridor on the 25th floor, talking to Benjamin on the phone.

"Well, the first on our list was Buckland's office," Benjamin was saying. "Could the money have been in there?"

"There was a painting," Ash said. "There could have been a wall safe behind it. And there could have been a floor safe just about anywhere."

"Not a deep one," Benjamin said. "The floor isn't thick enough."

"True. But if the money's in bearer bonds, it might fit."

"Can you go back and check?"

"He'll leave for dinner," Ash said. "If I haven't found the money by then, I'll try to get back in."

"Great," Benjamin said. "In the meantime, there are three

more places to search. The north room, the south room and the basement car park. What do you want to do first?"

Ash thought about it as she walked to the lift. The security around the north room was lightest, so it was the least likely. But she didn't want to deal with the south room or the basement unless she had to.

"The north room," Ash said. "Eliminate the least likely first."

"Okay. Let's do this."

Ping. The lift doors opened, and Ash stepped out onto level 24, the floor below Buckland's office. There were white plaster walls around the offices, and blue-grey barriers between the cubicles. The air held the burbling of quiet chatter, the occasional chirp of a phone. The carpet smelled like a new car.

Ash glanced around to check that no one was in sight. Then she reached into her pocket and extracted a black box with a 3.5 mm plug. She reached up and jammed it into the back of the security camera above her.

The box contained a virus that Benjamin had programmed. It would spread from this camera through to almost all the others in a matter of minutes. All the infected cameras would function normally – except when Ash came near them. She was wearing a transmitter on her belt which broadcast a high frequency EMP, tuned to the wavelength of the cameras. The virus made them susceptible to it, and programmed them to loop the past sixty seconds instead of shutting down.

From now on, Ash would be a ghost, not showing up on any of the security footage.

Ash plugged her iPod headphones into her phone with the converter Benjamin had made. She bobbed her head to an imaginary rhythm, moving just enough to convince someone she was listening to music but not so much that she drew attention to herself.

"You remember the floor plan?"

"Of course," Ash whispered. The right speaker was also a super-sensitive condenser microphone – Benjamin could hear everything she could. She could speak as softly as she liked and he would still hear her. It was like her lips were almost touching his ear, thought Ash. Gross.

"Turn right once you leave the lift," Benjamin said, undeterred by her assurances that she knew what she was doing. "Then take the third left."

"Already done it," she said as she turned. She stared up the corridor. It had the same wood panelling and dark blue-green carpet as the corridors leading to Buckland's office. It was empty.

Bing! Her headphones made a sound as Benjamin sent an image to her phone. It was the map absorbed by the vacuum cleaner, featuring Benjamin's labels and illustrations:

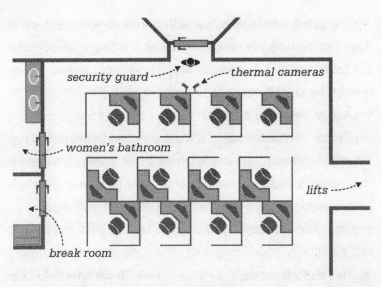

"The security consists of two electronic locks," Benjamin was saying, "one requiring a key and the other requiring a code, two thermal-vision cameras outside the door, and one—"

"And one guard, I know. I remember."

"Never hurts to double-check," Benjamin said. "Speaking of which, how about dinner and a movie on Saturday?"

"Nice try, Benjamin."

Ash peered around the corner. She could see the guard, a tall guy with huge hands, staring straight ahead. That was good. He didn't look too suspicious. He looked more like the type who ask to see inside your bag when you leave a department store – they're not expecting to find anything, so they're not even really looking.

The guard wasn't standing with his back right against the door, which was also good; there was a space of perhaps 60 centimetres. Ash couldn't see the camera, which meant it must be on the opposite wall, facing the door. "Won't the virus loop the camera feeds?"

"Nope," Benjamin said. "It's not attached to the rest of the network. And you can't block it from there, either. That's why they used a thermal camera. Heat can still travel through anything you could paint over the lens, so it will be able to see you. And you can't cut the power to it, either – the alarms will go off."

This one was going to be tricky. "At least we have the code for the door."

Once they had identified this room as a potential candidate, they had gone back to the footage taken by the vacuum cleaner. The camera's battery was good for six months, so it was still filming. They recorded the footage onto Benjamin's computer, then fast-forwarded to where it passed the door with the security guard each day.

Eventually they hit pay dirt. The vacuum cleaner was passing the guard just as he was opening the door at 7 a.m. He was supposed to inspect the room three times a day – once when he arrived at 7, once when he returned from his lunch break and relieved his replacement at 1 p.m., and one more time before he left at 7 p.m. The vacuum cleaner saw him punch in the code: 72269. They had waited for the robot to catch him in the act again, so they could be certain the code didn't change each day. It didn't; he hit 72269 again the second time.

Ash glanced at her watch. It was 4.43. Plenty of time before the guard gave up his post. She stared at his belt. There was the key to the second electronic lock, gleaming in the fluorescent glow from the ceiling. Part of the reason the north room was a candidate was because of the two locks. If the door led to an office, it might be key-locked. If it led to a server lab, it might have a key code. But if you were hiding $200 million behind it, you'd probably want both.

"I have no idea how you're going to pull this off," Benjamin said.

"You say that every time," Ash whispered.

"Towchi."

"It's pronounced *touché*," she said. Benjamin often mispronounced words because he'd only seen them written down. But sometimes he did it on purpose. Ash could never tell when he was kidding.

"Anyway, it's always true," he said.

"What is?"

"That I have no idea how you're going to pull this off."

"But I always do," she said. Benjamin always challenged her like this. Ash worked best when someone was telling her the task was impossible. "Shut up for a second," she said, "I'm thinking."

Timing, Ash thought. Timing will be the crucial thing.

The locked door was roughly halfway down the corridor, in a shallow alcove. As soon as Ash rounded the corner, the guard would see her. A few steps later, the camera would see her. She stared at the other end of the corridor. She knew from the blueprint that around the next bend was a short passage leading to a maze of offices and cubicles.

"Seriously," Benjamin said. "How are you going to do it?"

"You'll see," Ash said.

She backtracked, taking the other way around to the cubicles. A guy carrying a binder walked past her, staring curiously. Forty-five thousand, she thought. When Ash was twelve, her mother had trained her to guess the value of strangers by checking out their clothes, haircut and bag. Shoes were the best indicator; how expensive they were, how old. This guy had no bag, but wore a designer shirt and trousers. His hair was short and practical, and he was wearing running shoes. Clean and new, made locally rather than in Taiwan or China. He would have about $45,000 in the bank, minus some credit card debt, and maybe a rotating mortgage.

It wasn't until after her mother left that Ash realized she had always said "value", not "financial value". To her, they were one and the same.

Now, every time Ash caught herself playing the guessing game, she was disgusted. But she couldn't stop – it had become instinctive. A reflex.

The guy looked like he was going to say something to her, like ask if she was lost. Then he saw her name badge, with LEVEL 25 SECURITY CLEARANCE printed on it. He averted his eyes and kept walking.

Nice, Ash thought. This really is an all-access pass. What makes big corporations so easy to steal from is that there are so many people working for the company that it's impossible for anybody to know everybody else or everybody else's business. Sometimes you can just walk right in and take what you want in plain sight, and no one will stop you because everyone assumes you're doing what you're supposed to be doing.

There was a cubicle doorway peppered with Post-it notes to Ash's left. Clearly the owner of this cubicle was away today. Ash was in no danger of being interrupted.

She grabbed a rubbish bin from the floor and put it on the desk. There was a hole punch beside the computer. She picked it up, pressed it against the rim of the bin and clicked it repeatedly until she'd made a small hole in the metal. Then she started filling the bin. She took paperclips and pens and dumped them in. She tossed the hole punch inside. She scrunched up documents to make balls of paper, and threw them into the bin. She snatched a blue plastic binder off the desk, snapped it into pieces, and sprinkled them in. She cracked open a stapler, poured in the staples, and dropped the stapler in after them.

She grabbed a roll of sticky tape, ripped off a strip with her teeth, and stuck a glass paperweight to the inside wall of the bin, right under the hole she'd made. Now it was off balance; the slightest nudge would knock it over. She dropped the sticky tape into her handbag, along with a few A4 sheets of paper and a whiteboard marker. Then she picked up the bin and left the cubicle.

A minute later she was back in the corridor with the security guard, but at the opposite end. She placed the bin carefully near the wall at the bend. She stared at it with a critical eye. It should tumble right out into the middle of the corridor when it fell.

Time for the next part of her preparations. She walked back out towards the cubicles and turned into the break room. It was fully equipped; there was a stainless-steel sink, a huge refrigerator, plenty of cupboards, a few tables and a dozen chairs. There was no one inside. She took some foundation out of her handbag and put it in the freezer. Then she went to the women's bathroom.

Before she went in, she stuck a sheet of A4 paper to the door with the sticky tape, and wrote *Cleaning in progress* with the whiteboard marker. Then she went inside.

Ash took off her jacket, her blouse and her jeans, put them in one of the sinks and turned on the tap. The water rose quickly to cover the clothes. Bubbles floated up out of the creases. She turned off the water and lifted the clothes, wringing them out just enough to stop them dripping. She held her jacket over her head so that the water poured down onto her hair. Then she put all the wet clothes back on and left the toilets.

The break room was still empty. Maybe everyone had gone home early because it was Friday. Ash hoped there'd still be someone left to walk into her trap. She opened the fridge, removed the shelves, put them on the bench, and climbed in, shutting the door behind her.

She held her arms across her chest in the suffocating darkness. She needed to keep her core temperature as close to normal as possible, while still cooling the water on her clothes. She shivered.

"Ash, your signal is weakening. Is everything okay?" Benjamin's voice startled her in the darkness.

"I'm in a fridge," Ash said.

There was a pause. "You're kidding."

"Nope. This is going to get me past the thermal cameras."

"All that'll do is give you goosebumps!" Benjamin insisted.

"I wet my clothes first. That should maintain the temperature a while."

"You're in a fridge with wet clothes? You're insane! You're going to die of hyperthermia!"

"Hypothermia," Ash corrected. Her teeth were starting to chatter. "Hyperthermia is where you get too hot. And I'm not going to die. I won't be in here long enough to change my core temperature."

"And the guard? You think he'll let you past out of sympathy just because you're cold and wet?"

"I can handle the guard." Ash hugged her knees. "Trust me."

Benjamin sighed. "Just don't get hurt, okay?"

"It's a deal."

"Hey," Benjamin laughed. "Does the fridge light really go off when you close the door?"

The darkness was so complete that grains of imaginary colour were sparkling around her. She tried to touch her face, and wasn't sure if she succeeded – her fingers and cheek were numb. "You bet. I—"

Snick.

The door handle outside. Someone was coming into the break room.

Ash's heart pounded in her chest. If they opened the fridge, the game was up. It all depended on the kind of person who had walked in, and how curious they were. An average person might just take something from the cupboard, pour a glass of water at the sink, or take what they wanted from the fridge shelves, which were lying on the bench. But a curious person might wonder why the shelves weren't in the fridge, and open the door.

She screwed her eyes shut. She should have stuck an *Out of order* sheet to the fridge door. She hoped the mistake wasn't about to cost her $200 million dollars.

"How long have you been in there?" Benjamin asked.

She didn't dare reply. She was listening.

"Ash?" There was rising panic in Benjamin's voice. "Ash!"

"Someone's here," she breathed softly.

She heard the tap running at the sink. The clink of a glass against the bench.

"I just looked up hypothermia on Wikipedia," Benjamin said. "Most fridges operate at about five degrees Celsius. The human body can only maintain its core temperature for a few minutes unprotected at that temperature."

Ash said nothing. The tap stopped.

"You have to get out of the fridge," he said. "Right now, before you go into stage one hypothermia."

Footsteps. Approaching the fridge.

"Now, Ash. You could die!"

Ash gritted her teeth. I'm not getting caught now, she thought. Just a few more seconds.

The door handle clicked. Twice – once opening, once closing. The visitor was gone.

Ash tried to shove the fridge door open, but it was stuck. Air molecules shrink in low temperatures, so the pressure was sucking the door closed. She braced her back against the wall and slammed her foot against the door. It popped open and she tumbled into the empty break room, coughing. It was like falling into a hot bath. The outside air burned her skin and the inside of her throat.

"It's okay," she coughed. "I'm out."

She wanted to lie there on the floor for a while. It felt like it would hurt more if she moved. But her precious cold aura was already dissipating. Soon she would be visible to the camera again.

She opened the freezer and grabbed her foundation.

Then she left the break room, cold wet clothes sticking to her skin, and pulled the whiteboard marker out of her purse. Below the *Cleaning in progress* on the toilet door, she wrote *Use other bathroom* and drew an arrow pointing to the corridor with the security guard. She didn't know where the nearest other bathroom was, but people always follow those signs. Her handwriting was a little wobblier the second time. She was shivering in the burning room-temperature air.

When she reached the corner where she'd placed the bin, she pulled what looked like a dental-floss dispenser out of her handbag. It was filled with a thin, strong, nearly invisible elastic thread that was sold over the internet by an Israeli illusionist. Ash cut out a few strands of it and started winding them together. Her fingers were cold and stiff.

She tied one end of her elastic rope into the hole she'd punched in the bin. She stuck a piece of adhesive tape to the other end, and placed it sticky side up on the floor, as close to the centre of the corridor as the elastic would reach without stretching. She took a second to study her handiwork. Perfect. Her trap was nearly invisible.

She strode quickly back towards the cubicles, then froze. Footsteps, up ahead. Soft, whispery against the carpeted floor. Someone was coming.

Her level 25 clearance badge wouldn't protect her from suspicion now that she was soaking wet. She ran forwards, ducking into one of the cubicles, where she pressed her back against the wall, and waited.

Then she realized that the cubicle was occupied.

A young guy was typing at his computer with one hand, clicking his pen with the other. He was facing away from her. Apparently he hadn't heard her enter.

The footsteps outside were drawing nearer.

The typing guy hit SAVE.

A puddle of freezing water spread across the carpet from Ash's feet.

Goddamn it, she thought. I'm trapped! This guy's about to turn around, and I can't leave until—

The guy's phone rang. Ash stifled a yelp. He picked it up. "Hello?"

The footsteps passed by outside the cubicle, and Ash heard the break-room door swing open and shut. She slipped back out into the corridor.

That was way too close, she thought.

She paced quickly through the remaining cubicles, returned to her original vantage point at the other end of the corridor with the locked door in it, and waited.

She glanced at her watch. It was now 4.59 p.m. She guessed that she had about five minutes before she had warmed up enough to disturb the camera. But she wouldn't need to wait that long. At five o'clock, most of the remaining cubicle-dwellers would head home; but before they did, they would go to the bathroom.

The security guard was standing as rigidly to attention as before. He wasn't looking towards her, but he wasn't looking away either. He would see her as soon as she rounded the corner.

Beads of icy water from Ash's hair trickled down her spine. She opened her handbag, took out the chilled foundation, and started painting it on her face. Her nose stung from the cold.

A minute later she looked in her pocket mirror. Her mascara had run, her hair was slicked against her skull, and she was wearing so much foundation that her skin looked plastic. She looked like a Bratz doll. It'll take a million paper towels to clean this up, she thought. It had better hide me from the camera.

She slipped the mirror back into her handbag and removed a miniature pair of bolt cutters. She held them in one quivering hand as she stared at the guard.

At the far end of the corridor, a woman was looking for the other bathroom, having followed the arrow on Ash's sign. The adhesive tape stuck to her shoe when she stepped on it, and as she walked, the elastic thread stretched behind her.

Crash! The bin toppled over, spilling all the items Ash had filled it with onto the floor. The guard's head snapped towards the source of the sound. Ash slipped into the corridor, now outside his peripheral vision. She raced towards the locked door as quickly as she could without making a sound.

Keep looking, she thought. Come on, you big dumb security guard; keep watching the distraction. Just long enough for me to get behind you.

Five steps to go. Three. One.

There! Ash stood perfectly still, sandwiched in the 60

centimetres between the guard's back and the locked door. The guard's cotton and polyester shirt was only centimetres in front of her eyes. She breathed as silently as she could. Her blood thumped in her ears.

Seeing the woman pick up the bin and start to put the rubbish back in it, the guard turned back to his former posture. As he moved, Ash's hand snaked forwards and wrapped itself slowly around the keys beside his hip.

Ash was still for a moment. The guard showed no sign that he knew she was behind him, or that he'd felt her grab the keys. She eased the bolt cutters forward with her other hand and waited.

Having returned the bin to an upright position, the woman started walking again; only to have it fall over behind her a second time. She hadn't yet noticed the sticky tape attached to the bottom of her shoe, or its invisible link to the bin. As a second crash rang out through the corridor, Ash squeezed the bolt cutters, and with a soft *click*, the guard's key ring was shorn through.

Ash paused again. The guard still hadn't seemed to sense her presence. She slipped the key she wanted off the ring. Then she slowly inserted it into the lock.

She glanced up as she worked. The guard was watching the woman clean up the mess for the second time. Ash had to hurry; right now she was shielded from the woman's view by the alcove around the door, but once the woman removed the tape and walked a few metres closer, Ash would be spotted.

Pressing the folds of her soggy jacket over the keypad to muffle the clacking of the keys, she pushed the buttons through the fabric: 72269. Then she moved the jacket to the handle, and turned it very slowly.

The woman straightened up the bin and started walking again. She shot the security guard an embarrassed *aren't-I-clumsy* smile.

With a gentle shove, Ash eased the door slightly open and slipped through the gap. When she was all the way in except for one hand, she used the hand to withdraw the key from the lock, and placed it gently on the ground beside the guard's feet. When he saw it on the ground, he would see that his key ring was broken and, with luck, he would believe it had simply fallen.

Ash pressed the door shut behind her, turning the handle so the lock didn't click. Then she fell to her knees and took in a huge gasp of air. Her hands quivered with leftover adrenaline. She pressed them against her face, wiping wet foundation off and squeezing her eyes shut.

"Ash! Is everything okay?"

Still panting, Ash got to her feet. "I'm in," she said.

"What?" Benjamin demanded, astonished. "No way! Seriously?"

"Piece of cake," Ash said, slowly regaining her even breath. "Let's see what Buckland's hiding in here."

Peachey stood on the edge of the roof, staring down at the city streets with the wind rustling his hair as he contemplated his next move. Cars the size of chewing gum pellets trundled silently back and forth below.

Peachey kicked some of the dust at his feet over the edge of the roof, and it evaporated into the void beneath him.

There was no question of surrender. Even if it weren't for the threat the government posed to Peachey if he didn't complete his task, it was obvious that Buckland himself knew far more than he should. He knew who Peachey was. He knew what he looked like. He had somehow known that he was coming. The whole thing was supposed to look like a terrorist assassination – but if Buckland spoke up before Peachey found him, that cover was blown.

Buckland had to die.

So now it was a question of finding him. Only minutes had passed between the girl leaving his office and Peachey entering, so assuming that Buckland had actually been in the office with the girl, he couldn't have gotten very far. A trapdoor in the ceiling was out, because that would have led him up to the roof, and he wasn't here. Peachey couldn't see any signs of a trapdoor, either. He had examined the walls, and fired bullets into them – they seemed solid. That just left the floor, and while Peachey didn't think that Buckland had had time to roll back the carpet and lift the lid on a hidden passageway, there were no other options.

Buckland presumably thought Peachey was unconscious in his office, and that there was no more risk. Once he emerged through the trapdoor down to the 24th floor, he probably wouldn't be in a rush to leave. Trouble was, while Buckland was probably still somewhere on floor 24, Peachey had no way of finding out where, or for how long he would stay there. Not to mention the fact that Buckland might have a backup plan.

Peachey's phone vibrated. It was a Nokia 7250; one of the most widely sold models in the world. Another facet of his bland, unmemorable appearance. The caller ID was blocked, but he had a feeling he knew who it would be.

He put it to his ear. "Yeah?"

"Is Buckland dead?"

Peachey stared out across the skyline. "No."

Tania Walker's voice was icy. "Why not?"

"He knew I was coming. It was a trap. You've got a leak somewhere in your organization."

"You're wrong."

"I'm not," Peachey said. "He knew who I was. He knew who'd sent me. And now I don't know where he is."

"Then the deal's off. You won't get another cent."

Okay, Peachey thought. Time to put my cards on the table. "You fire me, you're not going to find anyone else who can do the job...Ms. Walker."

There was a long silence.

"Did you hear that?" Peachey asked.

"You think you can blackmail me?" Walker said coldly.

"I'll complete my assignment. You will abide by the terms of the agreement as they stood yesterday. Deal?"

There was a pause. Peachey glanced at his pocket watch. It was quarter past five.

"Don't break any more rules, Peachey," Walker said finally. "You're in deeper water than you realize. Find Buckland."

"Can you hack into the CCTV on floor 24?" asked Peachey.

He assumed that the HBS security cameras were not linked to any sort of modem anywhere, because that would compromise their security. However, he also assumed that the government had at least one agent on the inside. This person would probably be capable of accessing the security footage – but Walker probably didn't want Peachey to know too much.

"Yes," she said finally. "I can get it."

"Buckland was in the room directly below his office five

minutes ago," Peachey said. "When you find him, send his location to my phone. I'll take care of the rest." He hung up.

The lift was on the other side of the roof – a block of concrete with several sets of gleaming chrome doors embedded in the side. Peachey slid his knuckles across the yellow cube as he walked past. The colour was strangely hypnotic up close.

He pushed the button to call a lift, tugged his jacket straight, and smoothed his ruffled hair. He took a cigarette out of his pocket, neatly chomped off half of it, and spat it out onto the ground. Then he lit what was left, but didn't put it between his lips. If someone was in the lift when the doors opened, Peachey could pretend he'd just gone up to smoke – he wouldn't be given a second glance.

Ping. A minute later, the doors slid aside. There was someone in the lift; a man in his forties, with a cigarette already in his hand.

The man walked out and Peachey walked in, dropping his apparently finished cigarette on the threshold and grinding it into the concrete with his shoe. He pushed the button for floor 24.

"Those things will kill you," the man mumbled around his own cigarette, pointing down at the butt Peachey had dropped.

Peachey smiled, but said nothing. The doors slid closed.

Complications

Ash opened another drawer. No sign of the money. The tray was stuffed with documents about a jewellery company that HBS had bought a few years back. She slammed it shut. The next drawer was full of permits and ownership statements related to the HBS building. Another held shares in a South American mining corporation. Another was for tax documentation.

Ash shut the last drawer. That was every filing cabinet in the room thoroughly searched. No sign of anything worth $200 million. She allowed her mind to rest momentarily on the figure. Enough to pay off her dad's mortgage and keep the phone connected and pay for school fees and buy petrol for the car and even retire on, someday – if only she could find it!

She wasn't giving up yet. She still hadn't searched the room itself – the floor, the walls, the ceiling. Anything that might have a hidden compartment.

"Any luck?" Benjamin asked.

"Not yet."

"Damn. So you got cold and wet for nothing, huh?"

Ash glared at the wall. "And how's all that staying home and pretending to be sick going?"

"Ouch."

I shouldn't be mean to him, Ash thought. He's always been there when I needed him. Two years ago, before she had ever stolen, before her life included something beyond homework and visits to the movies, before she realized she was any good at anything, she'd come home to find her bed missing. And Benjamin had been the one who helped her get it back.

She remembered staring at her bedroom floor, baffled. At first she couldn't work out what was wrong. The dimensions of her room had looked incorrect, somehow. It was like looking in a funhouse mirror.

Then she saw her computer was missing, and that shattered the illusion.

Her first thought was that her dad had moved her stuff. Then she remembered he was out of town for the weekend. She ran out to the dining room, and saw that the TV had gone. And the DVD player. And in the kitchen, the microwave and the blender left gaping holes, exposing walls she'd never seen.

The house looked *clean*. Like someone had snuck in with a giant vacuum cleaner, big enough to ingest furniture.

Most people have been robbed at some point in their lives. Ash knew girls at school who'd had their houses burgled. But her *bed* was gone. What kind of rotten, greedy burglar steals a bed?

The phone had been snatched from the charger, perhaps as a final afterthought. She took out her mobile to call her dad. But as she was dialling, she thought about how much it would cost to replace it all. Thousands of dollars, tens of thousands. Ash didn't know how much money her dad had. She didn't know how well insured they were. But she had a feeling that this would be permanent damage. They might have to move house, somewhere cheaper. Her dad would have to work more hours, unless he could find a job that paid better.

She hung up the phone. She couldn't give her dad that news. No way. She felt like she'd swallowed a tombstone. Part of her wished that she could somehow arrange for him to find it first, pretend she hadn't been home since it happened.

But she'd rather he came home to find everything as he'd left it.

She lay down on her couch, which the burglar evidently hadn't been able to steal. And she did what every girl does in a crisis – she called her best friend.

The missing phone was the key, Benjamin told her. You can't track a missing bed. TVs and microwaves had serial numbers, but they were of little use for finding and identifying stolen goods. But a phone is a transmitter.

All Ash's stuff wouldn't have fitted into an ordinary sedan so Benjamin hacked into the Department of Motor Vehicles database and looked up the names and addresses of every van owner in the city. They eliminated anyone too old to carry a TV, anyone who lived too far away from Ash, and anyone living too close, figuring a burglar wouldn't work too close to his home. Since the robbery had taken place during the day on a Friday, they ruled out schoolteachers, public servants, bank tellers. People who were likely to be missed if they left work to rob a house.

They had twenty-eight candidates left. Ash's dad had taken the train, leaving his car at home. He had his keys with him, so Benjamin showed her how to hotwire it. He'd read it in the *Worst-Case Scenario Survival Handbook*.

Ash was behind the wheel, for the first time in her life. They drove slowly, but not so much as to be too conspicuous. They pulled over at each address, Benjamin in the passenger seat with the charger of the stolen phone plugged into the power source. He dialled Ash's home number on his mobile and got a "sorry, no service" message every time.

The call would never connect – unless the charger was within range of the stolen handset.

It was the twenty-third house. Scummy shingled room, curtains all drawn – ordinary and boring and empty-looking. A white van was parked in the driveway. The phone rang once before Benjamin hung up. They kept driving, parked the car a few houses down, and went back on foot.

The backyard was overgrown; spider-web strands of grass stuck to Ash's socks, rocks fallen from the potted plants scraped her soles. No animals. The curtains weren't drawn on this side; she could see her TV through the window. Her bed was propped up against the wall behind the couch.

She beckoned to Benjamin, who was coming around the other side of the house.

"That's my TV," she whispered. "That's my bed. This is the place."

Benjamin squinted in through the window. "Do we have enough to go to the police?"

"Forget the police," Ash said. "Unless they have enough

for a warrant, he'll be able to destroy the evidence before they get to it. *My stuff*. Even if they do get inside, and he doesn't run, he could claim he purchased it at a pawn shop. And even if that doesn't hold up in court, he's still only busted for this burglary. A slap on the wrist, and his other crimes go unpunished."

"What else can we do?"

"Beat him at his own game," Ash said.

They found an unlocked window at the back of the house, leading to a study. Ash climbed through, and found both her laptop and her microwave on the floor. Under the desk, there was a garbage bag with all her dad's DVDs in it.

A quick search of the house revealed that the burglar wasn't home. He must have had two cars. Ash and Benjamin found some clothes baskets in the laundry, and put the stuff in them. Then they went to the lounge room to get the TV and the bed.

It was weird how *not* weird it was, breaking into a stranger's house. Ash's heart was beating faster, but not in a bad way. Her fingers didn't tremble, her palms weren't sweaty. But it was like the tension of the situation had fine-tuned her senses, intensifying reality until nothing escaped her attention. She could hear the hum of the burglar's fridge, feel the minute sweeps of air from the conditioner, and see individual leaves rattle outside the window.

"What do you think he'll do when he gets back?" Benjamin whispered as they carried the mattress through the backyard.

"I kind of doubt he'll call the cops," Ash replied. Then she said, "How are we going to get this home? It won't fit in the car."

"Well, I've been thinking about that. You didn't get your phone back, did you?"

"Is that worth going back for?"

"No," Benjamin said. "So, maybe we trade."

A grin spread across Ash's face. "My phone for his van."

"Seems only fair," Benjamin said solemnly.

She took the van, Benjamin drove her dad's car. As she watched the other cars trundle by on the highway, headlights shaving away the shadows, she was in the best mood of her life.

The man, the burglar, was – according to the DMV records – unemployed. So presumably he stole for a living. But she'd been able to take all her stuff back in a matter of minutes. If she'd wanted to, she could have taken all his stuff as well as hers.

She left the van parked a few streets from her house, unlocked, with the keys in the ignition. It would be on the other side of the city by morning, and never linked to her.

She was good at this. Really good. Better than the burglar, and he was a professional.

Ash had finally found her calling.

As she was searching the north room at HBS, Ash reminded herself that she had Benjamin to thank not just for finding her bed, but also for her career.

"Found anything yet?" Benjamin was saying.

"When I find something, I'll tell you," Ash said. "Okay?"

"Okay."

Ash shoved one of the cabinets aside, looking for a floor safe. Nothing. Solid wood, no seams. She moved all the furniture in the room. The floor was clean.

"It's just that the suspense is killing me," Benjamin said.

Ash rapped her knuckles on the wall. Solid. Another metre across. Solid. Up high, and down low. She tapped her way across the whole perimeter. All solid.

She climbed on top of the filing cabinets, and pushed up one of the ceiling panels. There was a hollow space up above the room. She poked her head through.

Nothing but cobwebs and dust.

"Looks like you can cross this room off the list," she said.

Benjamin sighed. "Where next?"

Ash's eyes were drawn to a chute hugging the wall. "Where does the air duct go?"

There was a pause. "Down," Benjamin said. "There's a hatch on the twenty-third floor. You want to leave that way?"

"Why didn't I come in that way?" Ash asked exasperatedly.

"Because you would have had to climb a 9-metre vertical tunnel, 25-centimetre radius, with sheer walls of thick iron."

"Right. Got it. But I can just drop down that now, right? Is there room to get out at the bottom of the shaft?"

"Yes," Benjamin said impatiently. "It tapers outwards towards the bottom – that's the other reason it's unclimbable."

Ash wrenched the hatch off the air vent. A cool breeze made her shiver; she was still damp.

"So where do you want to go next?" Benjamin asked again.

"The bathroom," Ash said. "I'm hoping they have a warm-air hand dryer, but I'd settle for some paper towels."

Peachey squinted into the darkness. What the hell?

Walker had sent an MPEG of the CCTV footage to his phone, which showed Buckland leaving the room underneath his office, wandering through the corridors of the 24th floor for a few minutes and then going through the door Peachey had just opened. The video ended there. And now Peachey could see why – there was no light in this room. The cameras couldn't see. He couldn't see either.

They'd sent a blueprint of the room to him, but it was disappointingly blank. He could see where the walls were, but almost anything could be in the open spaces. It looked like this:

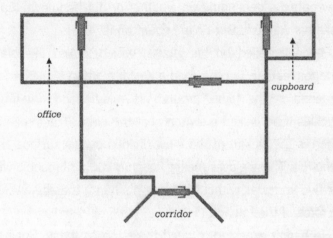

office

cupboard

corridor

No sound emerged from the blackness. According to the cameras, Buckland had walked in but not out again. That suggested that he was still somewhere inside.

However, according to the same schematics, Buckland's office also had only one door, and he'd escaped from there easily. Peachey gritted his teeth. Who knew how many trapdoors or false walls or air vents were concealed in the darkness?

This was a bad situation. If Buckland was in there, it could be a trap. And if he wasn't, Peachey would have to fumble around in the darkness trying to find Buckland's escape route so that he could follow him.

It's possible that he thinks I'm out of action, Peachey thought. Either unconscious in his office or splattered in the alley outside, depending on whether or not he knows that I broke his window. But I can't count on it.

Peachey pulled on his gloves, which looked like black imitation leather. But they had a Kevlar memory skeleton that hardened at the joints around his middle and ring-finger knuckles if he flicked a switch near the wrist. The force of a punch is the weight of the blow divided by the surface area of the fist. These gloves meant Peachey could hit people with just two knuckles without injuring his hand, thereby trebling the force of the impact.

He hadn't expected to need these gloves today. But he'd been forced to abandon his gun in Buckland's office. For now, he would have to do all his work with his hands – but at least they wouldn't be bare.

There was no point standing outside the door to the dark room. Peachey walked inside, and closed the door behind him.

His breathing echoed in the darkness. He opened his mouth wider to lessen the hissing. He listened carefully, but heard nothing. There was no indication that anyone else was in the room.

The floor was tiled rather than carpeted. Peachey walked slowly and carefully, short steps, heels first.

His knee bumped against a chair, and he froze. He'd made a noise. Had anyone heard it?

Click. A noise came from somewhere in front of him. It wasn't a safety catch on a gun. He knew what that sounded like. This could be anything from a door handle turning to a sticky-soled shoe lifting off the tiles. Or it could be nothing at all.

Peachey crept forward slowly. He hit the switch on his left glove, and it silently moulded into its deadly shape.

There was a wall up ahead. Peachey could sense it – his breaths bounced off it and came back to him. He reached out and touched it with his right hand – it was rough, like sandpaper. He felt his way across it to the right, looking for the door.

Here it was. Cold, hard, strong. Metal. Peachey turned the handle slowly and carefully. It wasn't locked.

Light! Peachey stepped quickly backwards out of the sudden glare. The door to the office at the left end of the corridor was open, and a light was on inside.

Peachey eased his head back through the doorway. There was a dimly lit office, but the map had failed him. It was at the end of a long stretch of darkness, interrupted by two small light bulbs. The corridor must connect this room to the adjacent one. Peachey redrew the schematic in his head to match the facts – it should look like this:

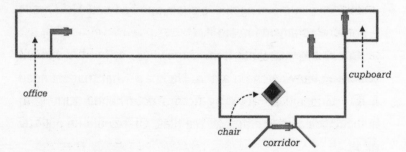

office

chair

corridor

cupboard

The walls of the office were clothed in shelves and binders, the floor was carpeted in a gloomy grey. Peachey could just make out a man sitting at a desk, typing on a computer.

It looked like Buckland. But Peachey wasn't close enough to be sure.

He crept towards the office, his back against the wall of the corridor. He was slowly nearing the light, and he didn't want Buckland to turn around and see him too early. He wanted to be able to sneak up behind him, put a gloved hand over his mouth, see the terror in his eyes as he realized that his life was about to end—

Peachey jumped back. There was another man in the corridor, creeping steadily towards him! He could see the silhouette; broad shoulders, hunched neck.

The man was standing in the middle of the corridor now, apparently aware that he'd been spotted. Buckland hadn't turned from his computer. If Peachey killed the intruder quickly and silently, he might still catch Buckland unawares.

Peachey charged forwards. The man ran towards him, fist raised. Peachey saw this, and at the last second tried to duck under the blow—

Bang! Peachey fell back against the floor, and scrambled immediately back up. It was like the guy was made of steel. All hope of stealth was lost now, so he ran forward again, hoping to duck around his opponent and reach Buckland before he did another vanishing act.

Peachey skidded to a halt as he saw his opponent up close. The man had his face. Peachey's face. He had been running towards a mirror.

So, the office...

Peachey whirled around in time to see Buckland wave from the cupboard. It had been done up to look like an office; Buckland had been behind him all along. Peachey's view was suddenly obscured as a barrier slid shut, separating him from the door he'd entered through.

The whole thing had been a trap. And Peachey had walked right into it.

A light clicked on above him, dashing all Peachey's hopes of escape. The walls and ceiling were concrete. The barrier that had sealed him in was steel, thick and solid.

There was a window in the barrier, about 20 centimetres square. Buckland's face appeared at it.

"I tried to deal with you reasonably, Peachey," he said. His voice came from speakers in the ceiling. "I offered you the most peaceful way out, under the circumstances."

Peachey clicked his right glove into shape and hurled his fist at the window. The glass was so thick it didn't even crack. Peachey's knuckles were undamaged, but the shock shuddered right up his arm.

"I'm not feeling so generous any more," Buckland continued, as if Peachey hadn't moved. "Not after you broke the window in my office."

"I'll break a lot more than that," Peachey shouted. "You think this room can hold me?"

"Yes. Indefinitely if I wanted. But I need you out of the way. So, in thirty seconds, the floor will open, dropping you into the building's backup water storage tank. You'll drown."

"I can swim," Peachey growled.

"I think not – you'll be wrapped in a net." Buckland shrugged. "For what it's worth, I'm sorry about this. You're smart, dedicated, presentable – in other circumstances you would have made a model employee." He sighed. "Is there anyone you'd like me to pass your goodbyes on to?"

"Don't waste your time," Peachey said. "Say your own goodbyes. I'll find you again."

Buckland didn't say anything else. His face receded from the window.

Peachey punched the glass again, but still it didn't break. He raced towards the mirror and hit it with a flying kick. The mirror shattered, tumbling to the floor in sparkling shards. There was a concrete wall behind it.

He had only ten or fifteen seconds left before the floor opened up, if Buckland was to be believed. Peachey's options seemed non-existent. Every surface was unbreakable, there was no one he could call for help and there was nothing to grab onto to avoid falling into a net, if there was one.

Tick tock. Ten seconds, if that. Peachey shrugged his coat off his left arm, but left his right in the sleeve. He jumped into the air, slammed his left hand against one concrete wall and pushed both his feet against the opposite one. His right shoe slipped, skipping down the concrete before catching half a metre lower. He adjusted his left foot and left hand to match, relieving some of the stretching of his joints. He hovered there, propped between the two walls, until the floor slid out from underneath the corridor, as smoothly as a sword drawn from its scabbard. Shards of the broken mirror tumbled down into the darkness.

Peachey had expected the roar of rushing water, and the foamy crests of waves below him. But as he watched the floor glide aside, he couldn't even see the water through the widening chasm. It was still and silent, an indeterminable distance below him. But he could see the net – it spanned the width and breadth of the corridor, about a metre below where the floor had been.

Buckland was right. If he fell into it, he would become hopelessly tangled in moments, and then, when he hit the water, he would drown. And his left arm was becoming sore.

Peachey swung his coat up to rest on his torso with his free arm. He pulled his cigarette lighter from his pocket, and clicked it a few times. A flame appeared near the nozzle.

Peachey rested the lighter on top of the coat. Come on, he thought. His legs were quivering with the strain of supporting him. His left elbow creaked. His palm was getting sweaty.

The coat caught alight. Flames licked up across the lining, spreading to the extremities of the coat. Peachey pushed it off his right arm and it fell into the net.

The fire squirmed outwards from the sleeves and tails of Peachey's coat as it landed in the centre of the net. The ropes and knots unwound as the heat fried them. Moments later, the net disintegrated into trails of burning string.

Peachey couldn't hold his position any longer. He released the pressure on the walls, and fell into the blackness.

He seemed to fall for a long time. Suddenly he thought that Buckland might have tricked him again – that he was actually falling towards granite or steel and that the net would have saved his life.

But then, with a splash, he was in water, freezing cold, like millions of needles forcing themselves through his skin. He fought the urge to gasp.

He kicked and pushed, and his head breached the surface. He sucked in air until his lungs felt like they would burst, then pushed it all out again. His breaths boomed around the dark cavern.

With a powerful freestyle stroke, Peachey headed for the edge of the tank. If he couldn't climb out there, he would swim the perimeter, looking for a ladder. If he had no luck with that, he would swim to the bottom and open a valve to empty the pool.

Buckland's voice echoed through the corridors of his mind. *I'm sorry about this.*

"You will be," Peachey grunted, and he slipped back under the water.

The water tank turned out to be quite large – bigger than the building probably required. It took maybe two minutes to swim around the perimeter and find the ladder. Peachey clambered up, tumbled over the edge and landed back-first on the floor with a *splat*. He lay there for a moment, panting.

The girder-ribbed ceiling hung a long way above his head, almost invisible in the darkness. The room seemed to

Peachey to be like a miniature aircraft hangar, with a water storage tank instead of a plane. He wondered if the room was normally used as storage space. Why else would Buckland have a room this big inside the building with nothing but a water tank inside it?

He flicked open his phone. It was dead. He needed to find a new one. Much as he disliked his employers, he still needed them to be able to contact him. He needed their help to find Buckland. Plus, he wanted to get paid when all this was over.

He stood up and held his arms by his sides, letting the water drizzle out of his sleeves onto the floor. When the flow had slimmed to a trickle, he swept his hands back across his hair, slicking it flat across his head.

He didn't have Walker's number, of course. But the SIM card in his mobile might still work. If I could steal another phone, he thought, as he prised out the SIM from the back, I could switch the SIMs and Walker could call me on the same number.

He stumbled slowly through the blackness, hands stretched out in front of him like the living dead in an old movie. Pretty soon he reached a wall, gritty and cold. He wondered what floor he was on – it had been a long fall before he landed in the tank. He could have descended as many as three floors by now.

He felt his way across the wall until he found a door. He pressed his ear against the wood and listened. Satisfied that no one was on the other side, he opened it and stepped through.

The fluorescent lights of the corridor were garish after the darkness. Peachey squinted and looked down – then grimaced as he saw the state of his clothes. So much for not looking conspicuous.

And my coat, he thought. That was a good coat. Buckland will pay.

There was a woman walking towards him, talking on her phone – a Nokia 7250, he realized. The same model as his broken one.

The woman covered the mouthpiece with one hand. "Are you okay?" she asked, staring at Peachey's wet clothes.

"Yeah," he said, rolling his eyes. "It's a long story. Excuse me."

He pushed past her, bumping into her shoulder. She gasped and dropped the phone.

"Oh, I'm so sorry!" Peachey exclaimed. He bent down quickly, picked up her phone, and handed over his.

The woman smiled weakly and put it back to her ear. "Hello? Kate, are you still there?"

Peachey rounded the next corner quickly, before she could realize that the phone he'd given her was useless. As he jogged down the corridor he clipped the old SIM into the new phone. He should have killed the woman – she might be able to ID him.

But he knew these corridors had cameras, and she'd been part-way through a conversation. If he'd killed her, someone would have come looking very quickly. It was one of those situations where covering his tracks would only make more tracks.

The lift doors were just up ahead. Following Buckland around wasn't working, Peachey thought. There was the possibility that Buckland thought Peachey was really dead this time, but Peachey wasn't taking any chances. Instead, it was time to set a trap of his own. Go somewhere he knew Buckland would go, and wait for him.

The foyer? No – too public, and the building had too many other exits. He couldn't be sure which way Buckland would go.

Okay. How about the lifts? Buckland would need them to change floors – he couldn't have hidden passages everywhere. If Peachey just rode them up and down, waiting for Buckland to turn up…he'd have to sabotage all but one, so Buckland wouldn't slip past him…

Peachey frowned. He wasn't sure how best to sabotage a lift. He could push the emergency stop after a floor and then climb out the ceiling hatch. But he'd have to do it on every lift, and it was only a temporary fix – someone would take notice immediately and start them up again when they realized there was no emergency. And anything more permanent would either require more engineering expertise than he had, or be even more obvious. He was trained to shoot people, not cut wires and fuse cables.

What about Buckland's office?

Peachey bounced the idea between the hemispheres of his brain, seeing if it would break. When he was in there, he'd seen Buckland's keys, wallet and briefcase, so it was likely that he planned to return. He wouldn't expect Peachey to be in there – he thinks I'm either floating face down in the water tank, Peachey thought, or following his trail like a bloodhound. And the office is nice and private, with plenty of places for me to hide, and an entrance to the fire stairs just a few doors down for easy escape.

Peachey smiled. Buckland's office even had his gun in it. Perfect. He could still turn the tables. He pushed the button for the lift and waited.

Detective Damien Wright got out of his car and closed the door. He hadn't needed a map. He'd lived in this city for nine years. And the HBS building was easy to find. You only needed to glance up to see it. It was like a golden egg at the top of the hill.

People pushed past him on all sides. The street was patterned with so many pedestrian crossings that cars tended to avoid it. The few that ventured in and didn't park against the kerb were forced to move in a straight slow line, one chunk of road at a time, whenever they spotted a gap in the flood of people.

Walking to the KFC side of the building, Wright saw that there was at least some truth to the reports he'd heard. There was a broken window on the top level of the tower. Looking down, Wright saw that there were shards of glass scattered on the ground all around him, sparse but far reaching. Even if he found nothing else suspicious, he should contact City Services and get them to send someone to clean up the mess.

Chances were that the answers lay inside HBS. Someone had got fired, maybe, and broken the window in a tantrum. But if the glass was outside, something had probably been thrown through the window, and he could at least find it before going in to ask questions. The first law of policing was to be observant. Work backwards from the evidence.

Also, he wanted to postpone going back to the station for as long as possible. The government had raised the terror-alert status, which meant that Terrorism Risk Assessment had operational control over all other law-enforcement factions. And they were insisting, as usual, that 30 per cent of the force stay on-call at their stations, in case an attack took place and they were needed on the scene.

Wright didn't want to get trapped in that 30 per cent. So he was staying away from the station.

He walked into the alley between HBS and KFC. The walls were scrawled with graffiti, the pavement was stained with years of grime.

The chunks of glass were clustered more thickly where he was standing. He looked up and saw that he was more or less beneath the broken window. He stared back down at the sparkling ground, wondering what had caused the window to break. There was no indication of—

Wright bent down to stare at an object on the ground. For a split second his brain couldn't process it. The context wasn't right. Then recognition came, sudden and cold.

There was a human hand on the ground beside the dumpster.

Wright whirled around, staring down one end of the alley, then the other. People walked to and fro in the distance, oblivious to his gaze.

How the hell did a severed hand end up here? he wondered. And where's the rest of the body?

The bones in the wrist were broken rather than sawn, and the skin was purple with burst blood vessels. The fingers were curled, like the hand had been frozen in the act of trying to grab something. Like it might claw his eyes out if he got too close. He shuddered.

You couldn't throw a severed hand hard enough to shatter a whole window. Could you?

Wright's eyes were drawn to a red spatter on the rim of the dumpster. He looked up at the broken window. Then down at the hand.

No. No way.

He stood up on the tips of his toes and peered into the dumpster. The smell of old batter and rotten meat hit him instantly, the way heat engulfs you when an oven door is opened. He peered down.

A corpse in a window washer's uniform lay amid the rotten waste in the dumpster. The man's eyes were wide with terror, and his teeth were exposed in a hideous grimace. His right hand was missing.

Wright tried to picture the events. The window washer falls from his platform and lands in the dumpster, hitting his wrist on the rim and severing it. That was possible.

Wright had thought that window washers wore protective harnesses to prevent that sort of thing, but all man-made equipment failed from time to time.

But how did the window get broken?

Wright frowned. The window washer might not have been on his platform – after all, there didn't seem to be one up above. Perhaps he had been inside the building, and he'd been thrown through the window.

He pulled out his radio.

"*Dispatch*."

"This is Detective Wright, reporting a probable homicide. I need forensics, coronial team and crowd control, over."

His radio said, "*Copy that. Location? Over*."

Wright gave them the address, and hit a key on his phone. "Belle, you're not going to believe this."

Ash dumped the last of her used paper towels in the bin and turned to the mirror. She looked more or less normal – her hair was a little fluffy, and all her make-up was gone, but her clothes no longer clung to her and her lips had lost their bluish tint.

She opened the bathroom door and stepped out into the corridor. She turned left. She wanted to check the south room next. Then she hesitated.

There was a man walking down the corridor away from her, talking on a mobile phone. It looked like Buckland. He was slightly hunched – not a conscious thing, just like he was hoping no one would notice him. And he was walking quickly. He disappeared around the corner seconds after Ash noticed him.

Maybe he needed the bathroom, maybe he was meeting someone in the foyer, maybe he just wanted to stretch his legs. Whatever the reason, he was on the 23rd floor. A long way from his office.

Ash pushed the up button beside the lift instead of down. This was an opportunity.

The doors slid open. There was already a man inside the lift, who made no move to get out. Probably $30,000 in the bank and a $50 note in his wallet, judging by his clothes – which looked slightly damp, although maybe it was the light. Ash recognized him as the guy who'd gone into Buckland's office after her. What had Keighley called him? Mr. Stone, Mr. Fry...something with one syllable. Ford, that was it.

Why was he still here? She hoped he didn't recognize her. She didn't want to get into a conversation.

She reached up for the button for floor 25, but it was already lit. Ford must be going back up there.

The doors slid shut, sealing them in.

PART TWO

Two Worlds Collide

The lift glided upwards quietly. Ash watched the numbers on the screen as the other lifts descended, taking the employees down to the car park in the basement.

Would this be it? Would the money really be hidden in Buckland's office?

"Ash? Can you hear me?"

Ford was standing too close for her to talk to herself without making him suspicious. She cleared her throat softly instead.

"I've been watching the news," Benjamin said. "There are cops outside HBS."

Ash's eyes widened.

"Don't worry, they're not here for you. But I think you should hear this."

A newscaster's voice faded in, mixed with the hustle-bustle of street noise. "*...five o'clock this afternoon, when witnesses reported seeing a window shatter on the top floor of Hammond Buckland Solutions. When the local police came to investigate, they found evidence that this alley was the scene of a violent murder. I'm here with Detective Damien Wright. Detective, what has led the police to believe that this is anything more than a suicide?*"

A new voice came through Ash's headphones. "*Obviously I can't present many hard facts so early in the investigation. But I can say first that it's police policy to treat every suicide as a potential homicide, and second that a typical suicide victim would jump from the roof of a building like HBS instead of through a closed window. There are other elements of the crime scene that are not consistent with suicide, and so far there has been no sign of a suicide note.*"

"*By crime scene, are you referring to the alleyway that has been blocked off by police?*" the reporter asked. "*How can forensics determine whether someone fell or was pushed? What inconsistencies have you and your colleagues discovered?*"

"*I can't comment on that,*" Detective Wright said, "*without *compromising the investigation, and for the sake of the family of the victim, who have not yet been located."*

"But you believe that there is a killer and that he or she is still at large?"

"I can say that we believe there may have been more witnesses to the event, and we'd like them to come forward so we can close the case swiftly and satisfactorily. As we speak a hotline is being set up—"

Benjamin came back on the line, interrupting the detective. "They're showing footage of the broken window. It's the window of Buckland's office."

Ash's mind was racing. Someone had been thrown through Buckland's window? Who? The report said 5 p.m., and she'd seen Buckland since then, so it wasn't him. Five was about the time...that Mr. Ford went into the office.

Ash's skin erupted into goosebumps. She hadn't seen anyone else go in after Ford, but if he was here, and Buckland was here, then someone else must have been the victim. And if someone had been thrown out the window, it seemed likely that Ford had done the throwing.

Ash reached casually into her handbag and pulled out her lipgloss and her mirror. She pressed the stick against her lips, and held up the mirror. Ford was still standing behind her, staring up at the screen with the numbers. He hadn't moved since she walked in.

She rubbed her lips together and put the items back in her bag, but as she withdrew her hand, she snagged the bolt cutters. She slipped them into her free hand and used the other to close her handbag.

So who the hell was Ford? What was *his* agenda?

Ping. The lift doors slid open. Ash walked out and turned towards Buckland's office. She heard Ford follow behind her.

Peachey wanted to walk faster, overtake the girl and get to Buckland's office as quickly as possible. He had no idea how long it would be before Buckland returned to it, and while he had no problem waiting, he didn't want to arrive too late. It was 5.25.

He gritted his teeth. This was turning out to be one of the most difficult, annoying jobs he'd done in a long time. He'd once had to shoot a woman as she walked through a revolving door because it was the furthest away from her bodyguards she'd been since he took the contract. He'd once had to jump out of a moving train to escape after a hit because the body was found too soon. Even killing Jeremy Quay had been easier than this, and Quay was a professional.

But still. It would all be over soon. He'd be drinking coffee across the street before he knew it.

Keighley wasn't at the front desk. That was good – Peachey

wasn't sure if his cover story that he'd left his coat in Buckland's office would be enough to get past him, and he couldn't kill Keighley in front of the girl without killing her too, and then he'd have to dispose of two bodies before Buckland returned.

The girl didn't turn off at the bathroom, or the fire stairs, or any of the conference rooms. She kept heading towards Buckland's office. Peachey had a horrifying thought – what if she had left something behind after her interview with Buckland, and she was going back to get it? Like her handbag, or phone. No, she still had her handbag. But anyway, she'd want to wait outside the office until someone came to unlock it.

Peachey didn't think he could come up with a convincing enough lie to get past her without arousing her suspicion. He'd have to deal with her before he could go in. But where could he hide the body? Should he drag her into Buckland's office and throw her out the window, hoping she'd land in the same dumpster he'd used before? Someone might see her fall – better to drown her in the spa and weigh her down with something…

Keighley wasn't at the other desk, either. The security guards were missing, too. In fact, besides the student, Peachey hadn't seen a single person on floor 25. Excellent for privacy, but suspicious. Where is everybody? he thought.

Is Buckland so confident that I'm either dead or about to walk into his next trap that he's called off all security?

That couldn't be right. Hammond Buckland was a cautious man. Maybe that was it – maybe his security force was tailing him instead of guarding specific parts of the building. Lucky for Peachey. Unlucky for Buckland.

He was nearly at Buckland's door. The girl was still in front of him, still walking slightly slower than he wanted to. Her iPod headphones were still jammed in her ears; she probably didn't even know he was behind her.

The girl reached Buckland's door.

She kept walking.

Peachey exhaled. Apparently her destination was further down the corridor. He was free to enter the office unseen.

Peachey turned the handle as the student disappeared down the corridor. *Click* – the door was locked. Peachey turned to Keighley's desk and touched the mouse. The screensaver vanished and a game of Minesweeper appeared on the screen. Peachey typed the combination he'd seen Keighley use, and the door clicked again.

He slipped on his gloves and twisted the handle again. The door swung slowly open. He peered inside. Everything was exactly as he'd left it; shattered window, handcuffs on the desk, bullet holes in the walls. He stepped through the doorway and started scanning the floor for his Glock.

Where is it? he wondered. I could have sworn I dropped it right about—

Thunk! Pain exploded in the back of Peachey's head and he staggered forward. His legs wobbled under him. What the—

Thunk! A second impact, and Peachey toppled over, the carpet fading to black as it rushed up to meet him.

Ash lowered the bolt cutters as she stared down at Ford's body. She'd hit him with the handle-end, which had a thin skin of rubber covering the metal, but she still hadn't expected to need two strikes to knock him out.

Her hands were still shaking. She'd had self-defence and martial arts training, she'd risked her life a dozen times, and she'd broken the law more times than she could count. But she'd never bludgeoned someone unconscious before.

Ford's eyes were only half-closed. His tongue lolled out against the carpet.

Ash thought she knew who he was now. She'd watched him put on gloves before opening Buckland's door – he must be a thief, the same as her. He'd been headed for Buckland's office, just like she was, and he'd managed to get an appointment with Buckland this afternoon, just like she had.

But Ash had never killed anyone, whereas she suspected this man had thrown someone through a window.

She patted down his clothes. He had no weapons although there was a holster for a gun around his chest. If she restrained him, and kept her distance, he wouldn't be able to harm her. She grabbed Ford's (although she now realized that that probably wasn't his real name) wrists and dragged him across the room. He was heavy; maybe 90 kilograms. She was short of breath by the time she'd dragged him to Buckland's desk.

She tried pushing the desk to the side. It wouldn't move. She tried pulling it. It still would not budge. Excellent – it was either way too heavy to move or attached to the floor somehow. She snatched the handcuffs off the table, and tightened one cuff around the man's left wrist. She snapped the other around the narrowest part of the leg of the desk, and jiggled it up and down to check that it wouldn't come off. It held.

The best thing would be to leave him here until somebody found him. She didn't want to be the one who called the cops – there would be too many questions she couldn't answer. Someone else would do the right thing; she had bigger fish to fry.

She left him on the floor and started checking the room. It had changed a lot since she last studied it. Shards of glass jutted out around the edges of the shattered window. There were seven bullet holes – two in the door, one in each wall, one in the ceiling, and one in the floor. Examining each one, she saw that there was steel behind the surfaces. The room was reinforced with it. She started tapping the walls, like she'd done in the north room on floor 24.

"Who the hell are you?" the man on the floor asked haltingly.

Ash emitted a shallow gasp. He was awake already. She kept tapping the walls, ignoring his question.

"What is this?" he continued. "You work for Buckland? You're a part of his next trap?"

Knock knock. This wall was completely solid. She started checking the next one.

"Who are you?" the man said again. "What are you doing?"

Ash kept tapping. Another wall cleared. She didn't look at him – she didn't want him to see her face too clearly.

"Did the government send you? Are you their backup plan?"

Government? Ash thought. Backup plan? Had the government sent him to steal the two hundred million for them? Buckland might have been right!

She finished tapping the last wall. No safe. She started across the floor, pounding it with her palm.

"Uncuff me," the man said.

Thud thud. Thud thud.

"Uncuff me." There was fury in his voice. Like he was used to people doing exactly what he said. Like even if she did it, he might throw her out the window just because she'd kept him waiting.

The floor was clear, too. She moved over to the fern in the corner and tried to shift it. It came free with a cracking noise, revealing a pipe that had come up through the floor and into the pot plant.

Weird. But too small to keep $200 million in. She kept looking.

"I'm going to count to three," the man said. "If I'm not released by the time I reach it, I'm going to kill you. Understand?"

Ash pushed a couch aside. No sign of a floor safe, nothing under the cushions.

"One," the man said quietly.

Ash turned to the spa. The water level seemed lower than the last time she looked, but it appeared to be a normal spa. She pushed the buttons on the side, and the jets clicked on and off.

"Two."

Ash stood on the rim, stretched up and touched the ceiling. Reinforced, just like everywhere else. She scanned the room, looking for somewhere else to check.

The man on the floor roared and lunged forwards, the

handcuffs rattling against the leg of the desk. The desk slid an inch towards Ash, and the man's free hand clawed at the air. He screamed again, a furious, rattling howl, and he reached back and grabbed Buckland's swivel chair by its stem. Veins bulging, he lifted it with one arm, swung it, and hurled it towards Ash. It crashed into the wall as she stepped aside, denting the wooden panelling and tumbling to the floor on its side.

The man grabbed the leg of the desk and tried to pull it across the carpet. It barely moved.

"I'll kill you," he panted. "You hear me? You're dead!"

Ash didn't make eye contact with him. The money wasn't in Buckland's office. Time to check the south room on floor 24.

"Doesn't matter how far you run," the man said, his voice low and threatening, "or where you try to hide. I will find you, and I will kill you and anyone else who tries to stand in my way!"

Buckland's keys were still in the dish on the table beside the door. Maybe they included a master key. Ash stuffed them in her pocket, and opened the door.

"You can't get away from me," the man shouted. "No one ever does!"

Ash stepped out into the corridor and closed the door behind her.

"Okay," Benjamin said. "Who the hell was that?"

Ash took a deep breath. "I don't know. I think he might be another thief, sent by the government to steal the money."

"A psycho thief."

"Yeah. A psycho thief who knows what I look like." She took a deep breath, held it, and let it out.

"I wouldn't worry about it," Benjamin said, though he too sounded shaken. "One hundred million will buy a lot of hair dye, make-up and new outfits."

"But what will I spend *my* share on?" she teased. She pushed the button to call the lift.

"Towchi. Where to now?"

"Floor 24, I think. The south room. Guess what I found in Buckland's office?"

"Uh, two hundred million dollars' worth of postage stamps?"

"Buckland's keys."

Benjamin laughed. "That'll make things easier."

Ash walked into the lift and pushed the button for floor 24. "Totally." She smiled, and checked her hands. Not shaking.

"Ready to be rich?" she asked.

"Heck yes. But there's some pretty serious security around the next room."

"I know. I was there when we watched the video."

"A camera, a lock and three guards," Benjamin said, "all for 20 cubic metres of space."

"I know."

When Ash and Benjamin had watched the footage from the vacuum cleaner, at first they'd thought that the signal was jammed when it travelled through a certain door. The screen always went blank, like someone was holding a sheet of paper in front of the camera. Then they saw a second vacuum cleaner, just briefly as the original one turned around. Thinking quickly, Benjamin ran the footage through a brightness and contrast filter, and they watched it again. They were stunned by the precautions Buckland had taken to protect the locked room on the south corner of floor 24.

The door led to a short, brightly lit antechamber, the ceiling, floor and one of the walls painted pure white. Any trace of colour or shadow would be immediately obvious. The opposing wall was a mirror, which was why they had seen two vacuum cleaners on the video. There was a camera at the far end, covering the whole antechamber – too far away to spray with anything without crossing the threshold, and it wasn't the kind of camera Ash could hide from after five minutes in a fridge. They could see the make and model number on the side – it filmed digital video at a rate of forty-eight frames per second and a resolution of 0.3 megapixels. When they watched the vacuum cleaner enter the room next door to the antechamber, they saw that the mirror was actually one-way glass, and that there were three security guards watching the antechamber through it.

The door the vacuum cleaner travelled through slid open when the pressure sensor in front of it was depressed. It was less than two metres tall and barely one metre wide. Anyone on the pressure sensor would be immediately visible to the guards and the camera the second the door opened. The door at the opposite end of the antechamber, the north end, was key-locked.

The guards each had an alarm button in front of them. Benjamin and Ash didn't know what it did. Ash thought it might call for backup, Benjamin suggested that it might lock the motion-sensor door, sealing the intruder in the antechamber. Probably both. The camera might perform the same function. Maybe something worse. There was no way to tell who was watching the feed.

The door at the south end of the antechamber separated Ash from her goal. There might well be $200 million behind it.

Ash stood near the door at the north end, looking at the pressure sensor. It was visible only as a square of slightly raised carpet. The door in front had no label or handle, nothing to draw attention to it. If Ash hadn't seen the footage from the vacuum cleaner of the glaring white room inside, she wouldn't have given the door a second glance.

Except maybe as a potential hiding place. That would have been disastrous.

"There's absolutely no way in," Benjamin said, challenging her. "Not this time. Not unless you're invisible, and you can walk through walls."

"No need to walk through walls," Ash replied. "I have a key." She knew Buckland would have a key to the door at the south end of the antechamber – the question was whether or not it was on the ring she'd stolen from his office. She was betting that it was.

"You're not invisible, though," Benjamin said.

"Not yet."

"So how're you going to get past?"

"Easily," Ash said. "I only wish you could be here to see it."

She walked past the door, making sure she wasn't close enough to activate the sensor. Then she went looking for the nearest bathroom.

She hadn't lied to Benjamin. She did think this would be easier than the north room had been. But she wouldn't tell him yet how she planned to do it. In the lead-up to a job, Benjamin was always dazzled by her problem solving, and the longer she postponed telling him her plans, the more impressed he was.

She smiled. Maybe she wouldn't tell him this time. Get

through the antechamber and never reveal how.

Ash found herself wondering what she would do after stealing the $200 million. There were things she wanted to buy, of course – a nice car, for when she got her licence, and a classy inner-city apartment, for when she moved out of home in a couple of years. In the meantime there were outfits and accessories, DVDs...

She frowned. She couldn't really think of anything else. And none of that stuff cost $100 million – barely one million, in fact. So to use Buckland's logic, if she lived another sixty years and never earned another cent, she would still have $1.6 million to spend per year.

If they succeeded, she and Benjamin wouldn't ever have to do another job. That would be stupid – if they had all the money they would ever need, then why risk getting busted? One hundred million each was enough to retire on, so they would retire.

At fifteen.

But after she'd bought the car and the apartment and the outfits and the DVDs, what then? Once her living was taken care of, what would she do with her life?

She had the sudden paranoid suspicion that Buckland had given her the lecture on greed just to stop her robbing him. She shook her head. That was ridiculous.

She pushed open the door to the men's bathroom. The

waterless urinals glistened silently. The lights around the mirrors cast shadows across the tiles. The room was empty. Ash crouched down, peering under the cubicle walls. No one in there, either. Not surprising, at 6 p.m.

The mirrors were screwed to the wall with 3.5 mm screws, same as in the ladies' bathroom. She took a screwdriver set out of her handbag, selected the appropriate device, and went to work.

Pretty soon the mirror was free. It was two metres tall and almost three wide – difficult to carry, although it was fairly light. Ash took a roll of duct tape out of her handbag and tore off a few strips with her teeth. Then she rolled up the right sleeve of her jacket and taped her forearm to the back of the mirror. Holding it like an oversized medieval shield, she left the bathroom.

She figured a missing mirror in the men's room would take longer to be reported than one missing from the ladies'. Maybe she was stereotyping. But she'd been pretty lucky so far today.

Ash walked up to the pressure sensor. She removed a Maglite from her handbag. She took a deep breath, and put one foot forward.

The door swished open. She heard it move, but didn't see it. She knew the camera was pointed at her, and that the one-way glass was just in front of her to the right. She knew that the pristine white walls were shining. But she didn't see any of these things.

Her mirror-shield was blocking the view.

Ash stepped slowly across the threshold, pushing her mirror forwards as she moved. To the camera and the guards behind the glass, it would look like the door hadn't even opened. Because everything in the antechamber was white, all her mirror reflected was white. She was invisible.

The door slid shut behind her, and she clicked on the Maglite. She had to wave her hand in front of the bulb to check it was on. Because the corridor was so white, it didn't add any extra light.

The silence was incredible – so complete that it was distracting, claustrophobic. This must be what it sounds like to be buried alive, Ash thought. She took a shaky breath.

She walked slowly and carefully. Her shoes made no sound on the white glass floor. She didn't know if the antechamber was monitored for sound, but she wasn't taking any chances.

As she moved forwards, she would have to gradually turn her shield side-on to hide from the guards. This would slowly reveal her to the camera at the other end.

She tilted the mirror so it was parallel to the glass. This exposed her to the camera, but only for a split second – she pointed the Maglite at it, dazzling the lens. Because the room was white anyway, the camera would now see exactly what it was supposed to. Nothing. If someone had been watching closely, they might have seen Ash flicker into view as she moved out from behind the mirror and raised the Maglite. But probably not.

Ash kept the light pointed at the camera, and held the mirror between her and the glass as she walked down the last few steps of the antechamber. When she was at the south door, directly under the camera and therefore out of its field of vision, she switched off the Maglite and dropped it back into her handbag. Holding the mirror steady, she pulled out Buckland's keys.

The first one was the wrong shape for the keyhole. She spun the ring and selected another. Too small.

Swish.

Ash's head snapped around in alarm. She'd heard the door at the opposite end of the antechamber open. Heart thumping, she tilted the mirror so as she could look back the way she had come without being visible to the guards.

There was no one in the doorway or the antechamber. Ash stared. Doors don't open themselves.

Then she heard a whirring and looked down at the floor in front of the doorway.

A vacuum cleaner was approaching her. She almost sighed with relief before she realized what would happen when it reached her. It would treat her like a wall and turn back – but the guards would see its reflection in the mirror she was holding. They would raise the alarm.

Ash grabbed another key and jammed it into the lock. The white door didn't open. She took another.

"Ash!" Benjamin's voice. "According to its signal, our vacuum cleaner has just gone into the antechamber! If you hurry, maybe you can slip in as it leaves somehow."

"I'm already inside," she whispered. "How do I get rid of it?" No luck with that key. The next key was obviously for a car, so she flipped past it and inserted the next candidate.

There was a momentary pause as Benjamin accessed the camera inside the cleaner. "Whoa, I can see you! Well, part of you. Is that a mirror you're holding?"

"Yes," she hissed. "If the cleaner comes too close, the guards will see the mirror! How do I stop it?"

"Throw something white at it," Benjamin said. "The guards won't see, and the cleaner will assume it's hit a wall and turned around."

Ash knew for a fact she had nothing white in her handbag. She was a thief – all her tools were black. Panic rising in her chest. She pushed another key into the lock. Still the door wouldn't open.

The vacuum cleaner clicked as its brushes polished the floor. It had almost reached her. She only had two keys left

– but if she picked the wrong one, she was done. There would be no time to try the other. The guards would see the vacuum cleaner reflected in her shield.

She selected a round-ended key with a square blade. It looked about the right size and shape. Biting her lip, she stuck it in and twisted.

It wouldn't turn.

She twisted the other way.

No movement.

She turned her head in panic. She had screwed it up! She was busted! She—

Pop. The vacuum cleaner's treads stopped turning, and it fell silent. It sat as still as a giant dead bug on the floor.

Ash stared. It was a miracle! It had broken down at the last second! "I diverted all the power from the camera to the transmitter," Benjamin said, "then activated my fail-safe meltdown. When I inserted the gizmos into the cleaner, I made sure that I could destroy them if I thought it was about to be opened. Sorry to keep you waiting – I just had to make sure that when I melted the transmitter there would be enough power to blow the battery."

Ash slipped the last key into the lock and twisted. *Click.* The door swung open.

"The guards will report that it has broken down," Benjamin said, "so you'd better get out of the antechamber before anyone comes to collect it."

Ash was already closing the door behind her. "Thanks, Benjamin. You saved the day."

"You think so? That's interesting. Perhaps we could talk about it over dinner?"

Ash took a moment to wait for her heart to stop racing. That had been a close call. "That was seriously unlucky," she said. "That vacuum cleaner coming in at exactly the wrong moment."

"Are you kidding?" Benjamin said. "How lucky was it that it was *our* vacuum cleaner?"

"True."

There wasn't much to see in the room. Four grey walls, an air vent in the ceiling too small for a person to fit through. It probably goes up to Buckland's office, Ash thought. A huge white box, roughly the size of a coffin, was the only object in the room. Ash allowed herself a small smile. This looked promising.

"Could this be it?" Benjamin asked.

"Maybe." Ash put her hands on the side of the box.

There was a clock with a timer, but no sign of an alarm. She unlatched the clasp.

The lid snapped open. Ash jumped back. Then she frowned.

The box was full of dust. A grey-white powdery substance that nearly reached the top.

"Well?"

Ash stepped back towards the box. "I've found a box with a clock on it filled with dust."

"What?"

Ash prodded the dust with her finger. It felt a little like cotton wool. She pushed her arm in deeper, searching for something buried underneath. There was nothing.

"Take a sample for analysis," Benjamin suggested.

"Okay, but I doubt it's worth $200 million."

When trying to guess how the $200 million might be stored, Benjamin had made a tiny scanner capsule for Ash to take with her. He'd suggested it might be diamonds, and if so, she'd need a way to check their authenticity. Ash plugged the capsule into her phone so it would send the data straight to Benjamin, and scooped it into the dust.

But her stomach was churning. This didn't feel right.

She stepped back from the box. She wiped the hand that had touched the dust on her jeans.

"Ash, get away from the box," Benjamin said. His voice was shaky. "Stand as far away from it as you can."

"Why?" Ash said, backing away. "What is it?"

"Don't talk. Don't even breathe."

"What—"

"Shut up, Ash!" Benjamin snapped. "I'm just checking something."

There was a pause that seemed to last an eternity. Ash didn't take her eyes off the box. She half expected a muscular claw to push up through the dust and reach out for her—

"Oh god," Benjamin said. "Umm..."

"What is it?"

"Put your jacket over your mouth," Benjamin said. "Breathe through it. How much did you touch?"

"Benjamin, what the hell is going on?"

"It's not just dust, Ash. I think it's anthrax."

Pandora's Box

Peachey wrapped his free hand around his wrist, just above the cuff. This was going to hurt.

"*Aargh!*" He pulled, and the cuff ground across his flesh, mashing the skin against the bones inside his hand. It got stuck just above his thumb. The girl had done them up tight.

He wiped the sweat off his free hand against his trousers, rubbed the sleeve across his brow to keep the moisture out of his eyes, and pulled again.

Shick. The cuff slid off his hand, and Peachey gritted his teeth as the feeling flooded back into his fingers. There were advantages to having wide wrists and narrow hands after all. He curled his hands into fists, like he was crushing the pain into a harmless paste. He rested the back of his head against the side of the desk for a moment.

He didn't have much time to waste. The girl would be getting away. Angry as he was at her, that wasn't the main source of his desire to kill her – she had seen too much. She knew his face, she knew what he was up to. Peachey doubted that she was calling the cops; she was clearly up to something herself, and would want someone else to do her dirty work. But she would tell her employers. And Peachey didn't even know who she worked for.

He clambered to his feet and stretched. He still couldn't see his Glock anywhere, and finding the girl quickly was probably more important than having a gun. Now that she no longer had the element of surprise, he would be able to kill her with his bare hands.

He twisted the door handle, and the door swung open. She hadn't locked it behind her – first mistake. He closed it behind him, and tapped out the same combination as before on Keighley's keyboard. The door locked. Now no one would come in and see the ruined office before he wanted them to. Control. It was all about control.

Peachey worked through his objectives as he ran towards

the lifts. Maybe in the movie of his life, they would flash up on the screen, silver and sparkling. Like his mind was a computer. He smiled. Smart and analytical, like a computer. I like that, he thought.

Objective one: kill the girl. Two: return to the office and hide. Three: kill Buckland. Four: escape. Same plan as before this unpleasant interruption. Just with one extra step.

He pushed the lift button, and a door slid open almost immediately. No one inside the lift. He stepped inside, and stared up at the screen. No way to know what floor she was on. He'd have to do this the hard way.

Peachey was an efficient and methodical man. He pushed the button for floor 24. If she wasn't there, he would move down to floor 23. Then floor 22. And so on, until she was dead and he could return to Buckland's office to wait for his main target to arrive.

The girl was a temporary setback. Emphasis on temporary, he thought. The doors slid shut, and he waited as the numbers counted down. He glanced at his pocket watch. It was nearly quarter past six.

"Oh my god," Benjamin said again.

"Stay calm." Ash's voice was muffled by her jacket. She'd ripped off the sleeve she'd dipped in the dust with her contaminated hand, and was breathing through the rest of the jacket. She was holding the arm she'd dipped in the box away from her and tilting her head to the side. Why am I telling him to stay calm? she thought, teeth clenched. I'm the one who's been exposed!

She tried to steady her breathing. "How do you know it's anthrax?" she asked.

"I examined the data from the scanner, and the picture didn't look like the Wikipedia image of dust mites. So I checked the anthrax images on a hunch, and it looks the same. Well, similar. I don't know. Oh god."

Ash didn't know much about anthrax. But she knew that it was a disease, and that it came in powder form. She knew that it was a popular biological weapon because it was fast-acting and fatal. She knew that once you inhaled it, you were a goner.

This was worse than getting arrested. Convicted. Jailed. This was *death*. By planning the Hammond Buckland Operation, Ash had engineered her own destruction.

"I thought anthrax came in envelope-sized amounts," Ash said. "I thought that was how weaponized anthrax was usually used. That's why it was such a threat – because so little could do so much."

"That's what I thought, too," Benjamin said. "How much is in the box?"

"It's full, Benjamin. *Full*. As in, to the brim."

"That's...impossible. Are you sure?"

Ash wanted to scream. "Yes, I'm sure! The coffin-sized box is full! I'm looking right at it!"

That part wasn't true. She was staring at the floor, like even making eye contact with the box could kill her. Like it wasn't already too late.

"Maybe...maybe that's how much anthrax $200 million buys."

Ash coughed into her jacket, startled. "You think Buckland bought it? Why would he put anthrax beneath the air vent in the room right underneath his office? That's the stupidest, most elaborate suicide method I've ever heard of."

"But he's not in his office," Benjamin pointed out, still panicky. "You saw him downstairs. And you said the box had a clock. Like it was supposed to open on a timer. Or maybe he was planning to sell it to someone else, like he's using terrorist groups to launder money—"

"We're wasting time," Ash said. "Is there anything I can do now that I'm exposed?"

Benjamin was silent.

"Talk to me, Benjamin," Ash said. "I can handle it."

"You need to wash as soon as possible," he said. "If you haven't already inhaled any, then that will stop the ones on your skin from getting into your system. But if you *have* inhaled some, it won't help. There are medications, but only for mild exposure to mild strains. It's usually fatal..."

The last word was choked off. There was a long silence.

"Stay with me, Benjamin," Ash said. "I need you!"

"I'm so sorry!" he wailed. "This was my idea, it's my fault you're in there, I was greedy and stupid and now you're—"

"Hey!" Ash coughed again. She hoped the stuff on her tongue was just lint. "One: it's not your fault. Two: I'm not going to die. You diagnosed me from Wikipedia, for goodness' sake. I'll wash. I'll get whatever this stuff is off my skin. But I need to get out of this room. Is the vacuum cleaner still outside?"

Benjamin sniffled. "No, they just took it away. The antechamber is clear. But—"

"But nothing," Ash said grimly. She picked up her mirror, pulled out her Maglite, and turned the door handle.

Hammond Buckland stared at the screen. Interesting, he thought with a smile. Developments I hadn't foreseen are popping up all over the place.

He hadn't expected Michael Peachey to be smart enough to head back to the office rather than following the clues that had been planted for him. He hadn't expected Ashley Arthur to disappear from his radar, and then reappear out of the white room looking like the devil was chasing her. He hadn't expected Peachey and Ashley to ever meet, and when they both walked into his office, he hadn't expected them to both walk out again.

For the first time, he wished there were surveillance cameras in his office. He would have liked to know what had transpired in there.

Peachey was supposed to find the box. Not Ashley. Buckland sighed. No matter how carefully you examine and strategize and think things through, there's almost always something you didn't see coming. Wherever there are people, there are surprises.

It was a shame. But the plan should still work. It just required a little...sculpting. A new facet, here and there.

And it was good that the police had already shown up. Peachey had unwittingly done Buckland a favour by jumping out the window. Buckland wanted people to sit up and take notice of what was happening at HBS. He wanted spectacle. But there was still more to come.

He picked up the telephone and dialled.

"Yes?"

"I'm about to initiate phase two," he said. "Are you in position?"

"Ready to go," the woman replied.

Buckland hung up and dialled again.

"Terrorism Risk Assessment, this is Agent Jin."

"I want to report an incident," Buckland said.

Peachey dragged the lift doors aside as they started to open and stepped out onto floor 24. This floor should be easy to search – no offices or closets, just a whole lot of cubicles and a water cooler. One kitchen, two bathrooms.

Finding the girl was what he wanted most. She was an anomaly, she was unpredictable. She needed to die. Buckland could wait – Peachey still planned to hide in his office and kill him when he returned. But if he happened to run into Buckland among the cubicles, then there was no harm in that.

Except for Buckland, obviously.

Even as he hummed an improvised soundtrack to his movements in his head, Peachey was becoming concerned about this part of his memoirs. When they were made into a film, he didn't want it to become too long – any movie longer than about one hundred minutes bored him. But this situation was too complex to be explained in twenty minutes of action and narration. And he didn't want the Buckland hit to be the main focus of the movie, either. He'd done far more interesting things in his life than this.

Peachey had been born in the Solomon Islands. He had

never known his parents, but now assumed they had been European – his features were vaguely Dutch. His mother had abandoned him, and he was raised in a shelter with several dozen other children of varying age and ethnicity. He had been thrown out at age ten for brawling with the other kids.

The first killing had been accidental. He'd been out on the street for two weeks. He was in a dusty back-alley, fighting with one of the other orphans who'd been ejected from the shelter, a big fourteen-year-old with close-set eyes and scars latticed across his knuckles. They had duelled with milk crates, empty beer bottles, bricks – anything they could pick up and throw, or club each other over the head with. By chance, Peachey had discovered that if you stick a bicycle spoke into the flesh behind someone's ear, it only takes a little pressure to penetrate the skull and kill them. Suddenly the fight was over, and Peachey had a career.

He would stab wealthy tourists from behind in crowded marketplaces, from a distance of about a metre, and then lunge forward and catch them as they fell. He would grab their wallet as he lowered them to the ground, stuff it into his trousers, then yell "I'll get help!" and run while bystanders were still in shock.

In this way, he eventually saved up enough money for a plane ticket to France. His plan was to continue with much the same work. But Paris had twenty million tourists per year, more than the entire population of Australia, and he figured the pickings would be better than in the Solomons.

It was there that he took his first contract. A woman saw him kill a foreign businessman with a flick-knife in an alley, and instead of calling the police, she offered him 10,000 francs to kill her husband – half now, half later. Peachey was old enough to know that 10,000 francs was a lot of money for an hour's work. He took the contract.

Peachey curled and uncurled his gloved fists. The corridors on floor 24 were almost empty. A couple of maintenance guys were carrying one of those robotic vacuum cleaners down the hallway, already taking it apart. Peachey stepped aside for them.

No sign of the girl here. He headed for the bathrooms.

It was time to start thinking about his contingency plan. Peachey sighed. He was pretty sure that the government would try to have him killed after he'd finished with Buckland. The situation with Walker was one Peachey often found himself in. Instead of paying him after the job was done, his employer would try to murder him. That way they were covered; there was no risk of him getting arrested and cutting a deal with the cops. Spilling it all for reduced sentence or immunity. And once he was dead, there would be no more pressure on law-enforcement agencies to find the truth. Case closed.

Peachey already knew that Walker had a source somewhere inside HBS – she had acquired the CCTV footage somehow, and she'd got Peachey into Buckland's appointment book. Presumably she could have instructed her source to kill Buckland, except that might leave a trail leading to her. Much better to hire Peachey, wait until his job was done, then put a bullet in his skull and walk away.

The low-risk course, Peachey thought as he pushed open the men's room door, would be to disappear after killing Buckland. Skip town, and lie low for a while. But there were problems with that. First, he wouldn't get the rest of the money. Second, he wouldn't be able to work while keeping a low profile. Third, there was the slight chance that whoever Walker sent after him would actually find him. And then Peachey would have to do more killing. For free.

Peachey peered under the cubicle doors, and walked out again. Trusting Walker to pay him wasn't really an option. Worst-case scenario, she would have him killed as soon as he showed his face. Best case, she would pay him to try and convince him he was safe. Then she would have him killed as soon as he turned his back.

What he needed was a dead man's brake. A mutually assured destruction type deal. He'd already started down that path by revealing that he knew Walker's name. Time to go a little further. He needed a situation where his death would expose her, but paying him would solve the problem.

Peachey examined his stolen phone. It should have a feature which would record all conversations onto the handset. He found it under SETTINGS and switched it on. Too easy.

There was a guard standing by the door to an office on his left. The girl wouldn't have been able to sneak past, so it probably wasn't worth checking. But the guard had a gun; a Beretta 92FS on his hip.

Peachey had decided earlier that the risk of killing a security guard for his weapon was too high. But that was when he'd only had one target, instead of two. The stakes had changed. He needed a gun.

The security guard turned to face him as he approached. Not suspicious, but alert. "Can I help you?" he asked.

"I hope so," Peachey said, smiling apologetically. "Can you tell me where—"

He slammed his gloved fist into the guard's face, and the guard's head thumped back against the wall. He slid to the floor, already losing consciousness as Peachey grabbed the gun with one hand and prepared to deal a fatal blow with the other.

A gentle scrape of shoes against expensive carpet. Peachey whirled around.

The girl was standing right there, mouth open, dripping

wet. Like she'd just climbed out of a bathtub. And staring at him like *he* was the one who looked bizarre.

Peachey aimed the Beretta.

The girl sprinted around the corner, and his first shot missed, a puff of woodchips bursting from the wall.

"Ash! What the hell was that?"

Ash didn't have the breath to answer. She was running faster than she'd ever run before. The other thief, the one who'd told her he was going to kill her, was hot on her heels. Armed, dangerous and, by the look of things, really, really angry.

With a raspy snap, another bullet hit a wall as she raced past it. She pulled her head down as low as she could without sacrificing speed. A minute ago, she had thought she had only hours to live while a vicious strain of anthrax ate her from the inside out. Now, she might have only seconds.

She didn't look back. No doubt the thief would be there, and from her limited knowledge of guns she assumed he had at least six shots left. Probably eight, possibly ten. Plus whatever spare mags he was carrying. Although he didn't have a gun when I knocked him out, Ash thought. Therefore the gun he just stole from the security guard is probably his only firearm, and I didn't see him take the guard's spare ammo.

Ash didn't think she could keep dodging bullets until he ran out. And even if she could, without the element of surprise she couldn't take him in a fight. He looked as if he was capable of tearing her in half. Ash's thoughts flashed back to his outburst when he'd been handcuffed to Buckland's desk. I'll kill you, he had said. You hear me? You're dead!

So that left one plan. Outrun him. Keep sprinting until she was out of his sight. Find a hiding place, wait for him to go past, then double back.

Ash was a fast runner. She could do 100 metres in 13.3 seconds. There was the chance that the other thief was just as good, or maybe even better – but she weighed less. There was a difference of at least 30 kilograms, and that would give her more agility. So in these winding corridors, she had the advantage.

Snap! A yelp escaped her lips as another bullet skidded across the wall. It must have nearly touched her. Her heart battered against her ribs, spurred by an even mix of fear and exertion.

"Ash! Are you okay?"

Ash didn't like keeping Benjamin in the dark, but that was the last thing she should be worried about right now. I'm dying either way, she rationalized. He doesn't need to know that someone is trying to speed up the process.

The stairwell door was coming up. Ash hoped the thief had

lost ground rather than gained it, because the door would slow her down. It would be a perfect opportunity for him to take a shot. But it was worth the risk – the stairs would play to her strengths, and if she didn't take them, she'd run out of corridor very soon.

Ash slammed her hand against the door. It pushed open with a groan. She threw herself through the gap, bashing her shoulder painfully against the frame in her hurry to dodge a bullet that might or might not be coming.

She didn't hear a shot. She jumped down the first flight of stairs, pirouetted on the landing, and started running down the second flight.

The stairwell was gritty and rough. The grey-brown stone walls were almost craggy, like the inside of a mine shaft. The stairs themselves were thick metal slabs that rang like the lowest key on a grand piano with every step she took.

There was a crash from above as the man shoved the stairwell door against the wall. Ash heard the crack of his shoes against the landing, and kept moving. Jump, turn. Jump, turn.

There was a ping as a shot from above hit the railing, and Ash snatched her hand away from it mid-turn. The bullet ricocheted into the ceiling, cracking the concrete. Bad news and good news, Ash thought. The good news is that he probably slowed down, or even stopped, to take that shot.

The bad news is that he's firing so regularly that he probably has ten more shots rather than four.

The floor 20 door swept past. Ash could hear more booms from up above as the other thief jumped down flight after flight of stairs. But he was falling behind. Her decision to take the stairs had been a good one.

Floor 16. Floor 15.

No more shots came from above. The other thief must have lost sight of her. But Ash figured she shouldn't leave the stairwell before he was at least five flights behind her. That way he wouldn't see the door swinging closed, and wouldn't know which floor she was on. She'd be safe, at least for a while.

If she tried to leave now, he would follow her out onto the floor. Too open, no cover. And there was always the chance that someone was working late – Ash didn't want to drag innocents into the line of fire.

Floor 6. Floor 5.

The crashing up above had stopped. Ash kept running, but the silence worried her. What was he doing?

Like the tuneless tolling of a misshapen bell, Ash heard the handrail sing through the well. It was the sound of the thief's shoes against the metal.

He was climbing down the inside of the stairwell, bypassing the stairs completely.

No. He was *jumping* down.

Ash looked up, and saw the thief's legs appear against the rail four landings above her. She jumped down another flight of stairs, and he dropped down another complete floor. Now only three landings separated them. She jumped again, and so did he. Now only two.

Her insides twisted up. Her vision seemed to scramble at the edges, like a fast-forwarded video. It was like being trapped inside a nightmare, one where she was running as fast as she could and looking for a place to hide but every time she looked over her shoulder the monster was a little closer...

Ash looked down into the well. She was only two floors above the basement, where the stairs ended.

The thief took another jump. He was one landing above her, and he could see her. He was still holding the gun, and he pointed it at her. His face was as expressionless as that of an artist choosing his next shade of paint, or a chef staring through the oven door. Like this was what he was best at, and he felt absolutely nothing when he was doing it.

There was no time to prepare herself. No spare second for a deep breath, or even a rethinking of what she was about to do. She reacted purely on instinct, her mind paralysed with fear but her body moving like a well-programmed machine. She dived sideways over the rail, and tumbled down through the centre of the stairwell as the bullet whizzed over her head.

Her organs lurched inside her. In the second before impact, she tried to relax all her joints so she wouldn't break or dislocate any of her bones.

She landed like a laundry bag filled with clothes – flat, hard, graceless. The pain smacked out across her skin like an electric shock. The air exploded out of her. But the adrenaline muted the worst of it, and there was no time to rest. With no more landings to run down, Ash ran for the basement door, ripped it open, and forced it shut behind her.

She looked around. A few dozen cars sat among hundreds of neat rows, mostly sedans, mostly white. Ash couldn't see anyone around. These cars were probably here for the night.

She balled her hands into fists. Where could she hide? He would look behind the support pillars. He would look underneath the cars. If he was a professional thief, he might even look behind the stairwell door as he came through.

Ash had only seconds to decide. Any moment now, he would crash through the door, see her standing there in plain sight, point his pistol at her skull and pull the trigger—

Ash ran. Towards the spots reserved for the company executives. The man might look under the cars, but he might not look inside every single one. She pulled Buckland's keys from her pocket, pushed a button, and heard the *chup-chup* of doors unlocking – the doors of a Bugatti Veyron.

Ash's knowledge of cars was limited, so the fact that she'd heard of the Bugatti Veyron was significant. She'd once tried to steal one from a media tycoon. Only three hundred were ever made, and they cost about $2 million each – if you were lucky enough to be invited to purchase one. The Veyron was a two-seater sports car, which could travel at speeds of more than 400 kilometres per hour, with acceleration exceeding that of any other land vehicle. It had a sleek spaceship-like profile, the strength of a light tank, and looked blurred with speed even when it was sitting still. Ash wondered why Buckland even owned one, given that he was chauffeured everywhere in a stretch limo. Probably trying to dispose of all that excess cash, she thought.

She jumped in, shut the door, and locked it. She lay down across the front seats, staying as still and silent as she could. She knew the odds of the man seeing or hearing her through the tinted windows were minimal, but her life was at stake. She wasn't taking any chances.

She heard the stairwell door open, and swing slowly shut. Then there was a painfully long silence.

Why is he still hunting me? she thought. Why not go back to searching for the loot?

She tried not to imagine bullets smashing the windows, outstretched hands pushing inside the car, gripping her ankles, dragging her out, squeezing tight around her throat so she couldn't breathe.

It didn't work.

A crash echoed out across the car park. It could have been a door slamming or a gun firing or the hard rubber sole of a loafer kicking against one of the pillars. The vast space stretched out the sound until it was completely alien.

Ash held her breath, listening for more sounds, but couldn't hear anything over her own heartbeat. She hoped the thief wasn't a car nut. If he was, he might be drawn to the Veyron like a moth to a floodlight. And if he pressed his face against the windscreen, tinted or not, he might see her lying flat across the seats.

"Ash?"

Ash jumped. Benjamin's voice was surprisingly loud in her ear, and it stripped at her already frayed nerves.

"Yes," she whispered. "I'm here."

"What's happening?"

"The other thief got loose. He got a gun from a security guard and chased me down to the basement. I'm hiding in Hammond Buckland's car."

"Holy crap! Are you hurt?"

"No," Ash said. "Not yet. Tell me about anthrax."

"You think now's the best moment for that?"

"I could be dead before there's a better one," Ash

whispered. "I'm running out of time, Benjamin. Tell me what you know."

Benjamin sounded hesitant. "I've been researching it. But there's not a lot of good news."

"Tell me anyway. I need to know what I'm up against."

"Okay," Benjamin said. "Anthrax is a virus that gestates in rotten meat. It's weaponized by a process I can't find out much about. It isn't transmitted from person to person, so you're not contagious. It presents in normal flu symptoms at first, and then kills you fairly quickly. Mild exposure to weak strains can be successfully treated with antibiotics if you get them right away. But you've probably suffered a fatal dose."

"What antibiotics do I need?"

"Lots. Large doses of several different kinds. But if you can get out of the building, you'll be able to get them."

"How?" Ash asked. "Where?"

"Well, I've been watching the news, and there's a TRA van parked outside HBS. They've sealed off the block, and there are people in hazard suits walking around."

"You didn't call TRA, did you?"

"Of course not. Someone else must have found the anthrax upstairs."

Ash shut her eyes. Someone else had been exposed.

"So you think that they might have the drugs I need?" she asked.

"It's unlikely that they already know what the threat is. And the chances are minimal that the strain is so mild that such exposure as severe as yours is treatable. But I think it's your best shot. Except..."

"Except what?"

Benjamin paused. Ash could picture his furrowed brow, his white knuckles. I might never see him again, she thought.

"Except that they're not letting anyone out of the building," he said finally. "They've sealed the surrounding area, and they're telling everyone in HBS to lock themselves in the offices and switch off the air-conditioning to reduce air circulation. Once the quarantine is complete, they're going to come in, find the threat, analyse it, and then start processing everyone for treatment."

Ash took a deep breath. "So you're saying that I'll be dead, or beyond help, by the time they're dispensing drugs."

"Well...yes."

"But..." Ash drummed her fingers against her leg. "But if I can get out of the building somehow, they might have the right drugs in the van, and I could steal them."

"They've blocked off every exit," Benjamin said. "The building itself is surrounded by news cameras. How are you going to get out?"

"You'll see," Ash said. She didn't know herself, yet.

But she would think of something. She had to think of something.

Ash didn't notice the moisture welling up in her eyes until her breathing became constricted. Her nose was running and her chest was tight and then suddenly she was gripping the handbrake so fiercely that her knuckles were white and the tears were flooding down her face. She tried to hold it in, but succeeded only in muffling it, so her sobs were only silent shuddering breaths.

There was no way out of this. The odds were insurmountable. And there was no one else to blame. I made my own bed, she thought, and now I have to die in it.

Ping.

Ash's eyes widened. Someone had come down in the lift.

And as far as she knew, the thief was still wandering around with the gun. She hadn't heard the stairwell door open again.

Her first thought was that he might put it away, give up, leave. Or at least hide until the person drove away.

But she had seen the intent in the thief's eyes. Not forgiving, not angry. Not willing to compromise. It was like his face had been set in stone, with a look that meant he knew she had to die, and that he wasn't going to let anyone get in his way.

Ash sat up, slowly. She peered through the Veyron's windscreen. The first thing she saw was Adam Keighley, Buckland's receptionist, walking out through the doors of the huge cargo lift. The second thing was the thief, standing behind a pillar, pistol pressed against his chest, aiming at the ceiling. As Keighley walked, the thief stepped away from the pillar in the opposite direction, so it was still shielding him from view.

Ash could see what was about to happen. The thief would wait for Keighley to be facing away. Then he would step right out into the open, level the gun, and shoot him in the back.

Keighley walked, oblivious. The thief circled. In for the kill.

Ash gritted her teeth. She hadn't come here to save lives. She hadn't come to take them. She'd come to steal $200 million.

But if she didn't have long to live, her last act wasn't going to be cowering out of sight while the kindly receptionist, who'd only had the job a few weeks, was shot. I may not have done anything good in my life, she told herself. But I am not a monster. This is my chance.

She wriggled across into the driver's seat and sat up. She pulled the seat belt over her chest, clipping the buckle in beside her hip.

She jammed the key into the ignition, and turned it.

The lights snapped on. The motor woke, like a sleeping lion.

Keighley froze. Behind him, the thief stared.

Ash slid the gearstick into first. It made a metallic click, like a gun being cocked. She slammed her foot down on the accelerator.

The Veyron blasted forwards. It was like being in a plane as it started up the runway. A second later, it was like being in a rocket as it blasted off. Ash's head smacked back against the headrest, and the motor purred as the giant wheels spun.

In preparation for trying to steal the media tycoon's Veyron, Ash had refined her driving skills in her dad's car. She was okay – she knew which pedal was which, how to change gears, and how much to turn the steering wheel depending on the sharpness of the corner. But nothing had prepared her for going *this fast*.

Keighley was already diving right, so Ash swung the wheel left. The Veyron took the curve quickly and gracefully, like a pro tennis player's backhand. The thief had guts, that was for sure. He wasn't even trying to move out of the way. He was crouching in her path, pointing the gun at her skull.

Ash was sure he couldn't hit her when she was moving this quickly, even if it was straight towards him. But she kept her head down, just the same.

Crack, crack! Two holes appeared in the windscreen, but it didn't shatter. The glass must be tougher than the polymer usually used for car windows. Ash kept her foot to the floor.

The car growled as it sped towards the thief. At the last possible moment, he jumped.

The car didn't lose any momentum, but Ash screamed as the thief slapped against the roof. Instead of the car hitting him, he'd landed on top of it. She looked in the rear-vision mirror as the thief landed face down on the ground like a sack of bricks, already in the distance.

Ash pressed her foot on the brake. The Veyron stopped immediately, without squeak or screech. There was a huge shutter blocking the way out of the garage, the kind that only raises when you hold a card up to a scanner.

Ash didn't have a card. She doubted the car could break through the barrier – in any case, she wasn't willing to try. If the airbags inflated, she wouldn't be able to drive it any more. She'd be back where she started; hiding in a basement with a killer.

She clicked the gearstick into reverse. The Veyron swung around in a narrow U-turn, and she put it back in first before blasting off again.

Keighley had vanished. The psycho killer was starting to pick himself up off the ground. She drove past him. She didn't want to run him over again. She wasn't a killer. Just a thief.

The cargo lift was up ahead. There was another *ping* as the doors prepared to slide shut. Someone must have called it.

Ash changed into second gear, and put her foot down. The Veyron zipped towards the lift, so fast that Ash felt weightless. The lift doors started to move. Ash gritted her teeth, sure that she was about to lose her wing mirrors.

The doors slid shut – but not before the Veyron had rolled between them. Ash pushed the brake, and the car stopped centimetres from the back wall of the lift.

She glanced in the rear-view mirror. The thief was picking up his gun, and turning to face her. The doors were sliding shut. The guy was taking aim. Ash flattened herself sideways across the seats, and the bullet punched through the rear window and buried itself in her headrest.

The lift doors closed, and Ash scrambled out of the car. If she didn't hold down the CLOSE DOORS button, the thief could open them again by pushing the call button outside and she'd be exposed.

She pushed the button. Dragging in deep, shaky breaths, she pressed her ear to the door.

Silence outside.

The lift started moving.

There was something very surreal about riding in a lift with a car. She hoped it could take the strain. But this was a big lift, with a maximum capacity of – she checked the sign

– 3 metric tonnes. She was probably safe.

She eyed the Veyron with regret. The bullet holes in the windows had probably halved its value. And there was no one who would repair it without realizing that it was stolen. So few had been manufactured that a teenager selling one was suspicious even without the damage.

But she wouldn't live long enough to sell it, anyway. Not unless she could get out of this building and break into the TRA truck.

The lift stopped at floor 3. The doors opened, revealing a man in a hazard suit holding an assault rifle.

She stared at him. He stared at her.

The moment hung in the air, still. Ash figured he'd expected an HBS employee, who he would have directed to an office to limit exposure. If she'd been armed, he would have guessed she was a terrorist, responsible for placing the anthrax. But she was a slightly damp teenager standing next to a bullet-riddled Bugatti Veyron.

Before he worked out how to react, Ash pushed the button for the roof, and the doors closed between them.

Looking up at the screen, Ash saw that hers was the only lift moving. There were others hovering at floor 14, floor 9, the basement, floor 3…

…wait. Back up. There was a lift on the basement level. And it was just starting to rise.

The thief was following her.

No swear word Ash knew was harsh enough to describe her mood. She'd been soaked, shot at, and infected with a deadly virus. She was stuck in a lift headed for the roof, and aware that whatever floor she stopped at on the way, a murderer would follow her.

She'd never done a job that had gone as badly as this.

If she pushed buttons for a floor, the lift would stop at it. The thief might think she'd gotten out, and follow. But if she did that and he didn't take the bait, his lift would catch up to hers. Then when she did get out, he would be closer on her heels.

She pushed the button for floor 17. She would try the bluff.

The engine of the Veyron idled quietly. She wondered if he would find her if she hid in the boot, or if he'd think she had left the lift. Then she wondered if she could open the boot from the inside afterwards. Then she realized she wasn't sure if the Veyron even had a boot.

The lift stopped at floor 17. The doors parted obligingly. There was no one on the other side. She jabbed the roof button urgently a few more times.

The other lift kept rising. It passed floor 13.

The doors closed, and her lift kept rising. Come on, she thought, staring at the screen. Take the bait.

His lift passed floor 17 without stopping. He was now only two floors behind her.

Ash pounded her fist against the wall. Okay, she thought. I'll get out at the roof. I'll take the stairwell, run down a few floors, then find a place to hide. He won't know what floor I'm on, and he can't look for ever. Not with the hazard suit guys searching the building for anthrax.

She wondered why the guy on floor 3 had been so heavily armed, then decided now wasn't the time to figure that out.

If she was hiding from the thief, she couldn't be looking for a way out of the building. She couldn't be breaking into the TRA van. She couldn't be curing her fatal exposure to anthrax.

Maybe she should ask Benjamin which was a more painful death: bullets or anthrax. He could look it up on Wikipedia.

Floor 24. Two floors before the roof.

A storm of coughs charged up her throat, and she doubled over, hacking and spitting. The noise bounced off the walls of the lift. Her throat was scraped raw by the force. Her nose ran, and she wiped it on her sleeve.

Flu symptoms. The virus was taking hold.

Ash glanced in the mirror on the wall of the lift. She barely recognized herself. Sweaty, hollow-eyed from the fluorescent lighting – scared. But she'd heard people talk about a determined chin, and she now thought she understood. Her jaw was set. Her teeth were clenched. It was a look that said *If I'm going down, I'm going down fighting.*

Floor 25. The thief was on floor 23. Ash climbed back into the Veyron and shut the door. She shifted it to neutral and revved the accelerator, just to hear how loud a $2 million engine could scream. The lift walls vibrated as Ash gripped the steering wheel.

The lift eased to a halt and *ping*ed. The doors parted, and the light of the setting sun poured in. The yellow cube sparkled hypnotically. Ash reversed the car out of the lift, curved it into another U-turn, and clicked the gearstick into first.

The car was facing the building on the other side of the street. It wasn't as high as HBS.

"Benjamin, are you watching the news?" Ash asked.

"Yeah. They're—"

"I don't care what they're doing. But it's live, right?"

"Yeah, why?"

"Keep watching," she said. She buckled her seat belt, and revved the engine again. "If I don't make it...I've loved working with you. You know that, right?"

"Ash." Benjamin's voice was low. "What are you doing?"

"You'll see," she said. She checked her hands. Not shaking.

Ping. The other lift had reached the roof. Ash took a deep breath, and hit the accelerator.

The Veyron zoomed forwards. The wind blustered at it, but like the creature of extraordinary power it was, it shrugged it off.

Ash heard the crack of gunshots. Puffs of concrete dust surrounded the car suddenly, like heavy rain in the desert. A shot clinked off the yellow cube.

One hit the rear passenger-side tyre.

Ash heard a sudden thuddering from behind her, and the car swooped left. She twisted the steering wheel to correct the car's trajectory, fighting for control. The gunshots were still coming. The edge was approaching fast.

The wheels spun and the car leaped forwards. Ash pulled her head down while trying to keep the nose of the Veyron pointed at the building opposite and the guy shot out another tyre and the car went into a spin at 250 kilometres per hour and it was about to reach the edge and this was a bad idea and the wheels hit the lip of the roof and this was a bad idea she was going to die she was going to—

Contingencies

Wright stared up into the sky as the car flew across the street, twenty-five storeys above him. It actually flew, like a matchbox car someone had hurled across a room. It spun and tumbled and barrelled, silhouetted against the evening sky, and for a split second, he actually thought it would make it; that it would land right-side up on the roof of the building opposite.

The crowd down below were staring up with him. No one screaming, no one running. It was like their voices had dried up, like the flying car was a pocket watch swung in front of their eyes to hypnotize them. There was no time to feel anything more than astonishment. The camera operators behind the roadblock barely had time to swing their lenses up and capture the moment.

The car didn't make it to the opposite roof. It crashed through one of the giant windows of the building two floors from the top and disappeared from view. It hit the glass so fast that the pane was shoved inward, and not a single shard fell down to the street.

After a few seconds of dazed silence, a wall of people ran towards the roadblocks. Most of them were running backwards, stumbling over each other and themselves, still watching the sky like there might be more to see. Like fireworks might explode on the roof, all part of the show.

Wright squinted. Actually, there was something up there. On top of the HBS building there was a silhouette of a man, staring across the street at the hole in the glass the car had made. Then he turned away and stepped out of sight.

Wright was getting increasingly frustrated. He hadn't told the news crew this, but after calling in the homicide, he'd tried to go into HBS to examine the office with the broken window and question the remaining employees. And he hadn't been allowed in. A big white van had appeared in front of HBS, and a gloved hand had pressed against his chest as he approached the door.

"Detective Wright," he began, waving the badge, before looking at the woman who'd stopped him. She was dressed in a white hazard suit, complete with a hood, gas mask and visor.

"I'm sorry, sir, I can't let you go in there," she said.

Wright stared at her. He kept his gaze even. "There's been a homicide, and everyone in that building is under suspicion. I don't know who you are, but—"

"Danni Braid, Terrorism Risk Assessment," she obliged. "And I can't let you go in there. We've had a report of a biological weapon being deployed inside the HBS building, and we have been authorized to stop anyone entering the building."

"My team needs to question those people," Wright insisted.

The woman shrugged. "With respect, sir, they're not going anywhere. No one is allowed to leave the building either. And because you and your team are already inside the safety perimeter..."

Wright turned and saw that a roadblock had gone up, with city cops on the other side holding the crowds back. There were five more people in hazard suits climbing out of the van and approaching the building.

"I'm afraid I can't let you leave either," the woman said. "Sir."

So Wright had gone to the KFC to question the workers there instead. The manager didn't speak much English, and only managed to convey that he was terrified, as if he feared he would be fired for allowing corpses to be placed in a company dumpster. The other employees were all kids, barely teenagers. Greasy boys and made-up girls, who found the discovery of bodies nearby "cool" and "gross" respectively.

It's always the same with people who never knew the victims, Wright had thought. In large groups, they pretend to care. Most of them. But you see through it right away; they're just treating it as a surprise interruption to their day. Like a power outage or a fire drill. They're either pleased or annoyed about it, depending on how much they hate their jobs, but that's not the same as caring.

He felt just as detached. But he could blame years of detective work in a big city for desensitizing him. If he let the presence of death get to him, he'd have gone mad long ago.

Wright had been walking back to his team, preparing to explain the situation, when the Bugatti Veyron flew across the street above their heads.

Now, he turned to watch the panicking crowd. There were the people inside the quarantine zone who were trying desperately to get out, and the lunatics outside who wanted even more desperately to get in. The police at the roadblocks were doing a good job of holding them back, on both sides.

Wright saw a kid holding up his phone to the sky, recording video footage of the two buildings, with a kind of glazed hopefulness in his eyes, praying for more. It would be on YouTube by the end of the day, thought Wright.

The detective's phone rang, and he answered it. "Yeah?"

"Damien," Belle said, "the prints are back. Brace yourself."

Belle had been Wright's partner for two years; since his old partner retired and hers got shot in the leg. She was a lousy driver and too cynical to play for political advantage at the station, but she was smart. Much smarter than him, he believed. Thanks to his eye for details and her photographic memory, they made a formidable team.

"Did you see it?" Wright said. "Is there a TV near you?"

"What? What are you talking about?"

"Nothing." He'd get to the flying car later. The prints on the body were important. "Who's our dead guy?"

"No idea."

"He's never been printed?" That was unusual. Anyone who'd ever been questioned by the police or had a police check, anyone who'd ever worked in any way for the government and anyone who'd needed to prove their identity to various departments or companies in various states would have been printed. The people who didn't have their prints on the national database were in the minority.

"They were on file," Belle said.

"So you're saying that the prints have been found at other crime scenes, but the crimes were never solved?" If the window washer was a criminal...

"Nope. I'm saying that the database wouldn't let me access his personnel file. Classified."

Wright glared at the HBS foyer entrance. "No way."

"Yes way," Belle said. "Our John Doe is either in the witness protection scheme, on the run from the federal police, or, more likely—"

"A government agent," Wright finished. "Working for TRA, or maybe a covert branch of some other law-enforcement department."

"So basically, we're screwed."

She was right. Whatever's going on, Wright thought, there are major players and it involves terrorism, the government, and possibly corruption. Best case scenario, I get taken off the case because it's in TRA's jurisdiction. Worst case scenario, I never work out what's going on because too many details are classified.

Why would a government agent be washing windows at HBS?

"Oh god," Belle said. "Are you watching this?"

"Watching what?"

"There's a car jumping across... Unbelievable! You have to see this. I'll record it."

Wright pressed his fingers against his temples. "I've seen it," he said. "I was there. It's all connected, somehow."

There was really only one thing he could do. He started walking towards the roadblock.

"This is the weirdest case I've seen in a long time," Belle was saying. "Do you have a working theory?"

"Yeah," Wright said. "People are killing each other, and people who outrank us are letting them do it."

"The high court might want something more specific. It's hard to win a case *against* 'people'."

"I've only been on the scene an hour," Wright said. "Give me time."

A city cop at the roadblock was barring his way. "I need you to stay back, sir."

Wright flashed his badge. "Detective Damien Wright. Who's in charge?"

"I am," the cop said. "But I can't let you through, no matter who you are."

"Not asking you to," Wright said. "You've got your hands full here, and the TRA guys are busy keeping the HBS building sealed and checking out the inside. My whole team is stuck here, including forensics and photographers. We're going to enter the building opposite and check out the crash site for that car."

"I've been instructed to—"

"Keep everyone inside the perimeter, I know. The building is inside the perimeter."

The cop seemed reluctant. "I've sent for backup to do that."

"I wasn't asking," Wright said. "I outrank you." He turned away and started walking towards the building with the gaping hole in it. He stuck his fingers in his mouth and whistled to get his team's attention, then he beckoned. "Follow me."

They ran towards him. I'll get to the bottom of this, he thought, staring up at the broken window. This is what I do.

Ash woke up before her eyes opened. They felt gluey and tingly, like someone had taped them shut with Post-it notes. It took her a moment to rewind her memory enough to catch all the important facts. Her name was Ashley Arthur. She was fifteen. She lived with her dad at 146 East Park Way. She was a thief.

And the last thing that she remembered was driving a Bugatti Veyron off the roof of Hammond Buckland Solutions headquarters.

She opened her eyes. Incredibly, the car was still running; the engine purred as smoothly as if nothing had happened. The inside of the roof looked like a crisp packet that had been scrunched up and then stretched out again. The windscreen was still in one piece, but opaqued with cracks. So were all the windows. The only way she could tell the car was upside down was that her hair was touching the roof and her head hurt. All her blood had drained into it.

Ash took her foot off the accelerator, and the wheels wound themselves down to a stop. While the Veyron had survived the crash better than perhaps any other car in the world would have, she suddenly realized that she was incredibly lucky it had landed upside down. If the wheels had been touching the floor and still spinning, the car might have kept going right through the walls and out the other side of the building.

Ash unbuckled her seat belt and fell immediately against the roof. Storm clouds of pain thundered through her entire body, squeezing every limb and twisting every bone. Her neck felt as wide as her shoulders.

"Oh man," she whispered. "That was a dumb idea."

The iPod headphones had come out of her ears. Her arm crackled as she reached out to get them.

"Ash! Ash! Talk to me, damn it!"

"Hey, Benjamin," she said. She tried to focus her eyes on the steering wheel, but it was too close to her face. "Did you see me on TV?"

"Thank god," Benjamin said. "Of course I saw it. It was hard to miss."

"Am I identifiable?"

"No. Motion blur, plus poor resolution, plus tinted windows – don't worry about it. Are you hurt?"

"Cuts and bruises," Ash said. "Well, bruises."

"Can you move?"

"Yeah."

"Then start moving." Benjamin's voice was grim. "A whole bunch of cops just walked into the apartment building."

Ash frowned. "What? Why?"

"Because they just saw a car fly into it! Move it, Ash. Pay attention. Cops are coming. You need to get out of there."

Ash shook her head. It hurt. "Cops. Coming. Move. Got it."

She pulled the door handle. The door wouldn't open. Ash shoved it as hard as she could, but the lock must have been twisted. She braced her feet against the passenger door and tried again.

The passenger door popped open instead. Ash wriggled out that way.

She knew she had to hurry, but she couldn't help pausing for a moment to survey the carnage. Buckland's bullet-punctured office was nothing compared to this.

The Veyron had landed on a four-poster bed, snapping all four legs and crushing the frame against the dented wall. Walking across the floor was like walking through a barn, with broken glass and mattress stuffing instead of hay. Two jagged halves of a flat-screen TV were on opposite sides of the room.

And the car itself looked a lot worse than it had from inside. The bonnet had buckled, exposing the grey cylinders inside, the bullet-torn tyres sagged behind their crumpled hubcaps, and the rear spoiler was now three miniature rear spoilers. Two million dollars of automotive glory had become worthless scrap metal in a matter of seconds.

Ash tore her gaze away, shoved open the door, and stumbled out into the corridor. Soft cream carpets, cheese-coloured wallpaper: classy apartment accommodation. There was a sign that said LIFTS, and she followed the arrow. There were grey sliding doors up ahead. Then she checked the red LED screen beside them, and saw that a lift was already on its way up.

She staggered backwards, looking for a different lift, or some fire stairs. There was no sign of another way down, and the corridor was long and straight. The cops would see her as soon as the lift doors opened.

There was a janitor's closet. She ripped the door open, tumbled inside, and slammed it shut behind her. A bucket with a mop in it bounced against the floor as she tripped over it. She sat down in the corner of the closet rather than standing or crouching. Thief's instinct: if you're going to have to be really quiet for what might be a really long time, make sure you're comfortable first.

There was still a ringing in her ears, like a thousand tiny people screaming "MEEEEEE". In the silence of the closet it was painfully loud.

Her nose was running again, and her eyes were sore. How long was I unconscious? she wondered. How long have I got to find the anthrax antidote?

A muffled beep wafted in under the door, and Ash tried not to breathe. The lift with the cops in it had arrived. The floor had seemed deserted – maybe everyone had been evacuated when the TRA team arrived, although Benjamin said they had sealed off the whole block, so Ash figured this building was probably still inside the quarantine zone. More likely all the occupants had fled this floor when they heard the crash. Either way, it was lucky no one had been in the room when the Veyron flew through the window.

Footsteps outside the closet door. Quick, but measured. The sound of four or five people trying to find something quickly.

Ash heard someone kick in a door. The steely crack of the lock tearing through the frame.

"We don't have a warrant," someone said. Male. Young-sounding. "Think we should be destroying property?"

"We also have no way of getting a lock-release gun or

master key without violating the quarantine," a female voice replied. Ash heard another door crunch open. "And besides, you think anyone will care about some broken locks after the damage that car must have done?"

"What do you think we'll find?" a third voice asked. Male. Older than the first guy. "Surely no one could have been inside that car."

"Well, we'll see, won't we?" the young man said. *Bang. Crack.* "Found it."

"Whoa." The woman again. "What a mess."

Their voices were quieter now that they were in the apartment. Ash shut her eyes, trying to focus on sound alone. She heard the click of cameras. Broken glass tinkled as feet shuffled through it.

"Like I said. No one in the car," the woman said.

"Oh my god," said the young guy. "That's a Bugatti Veyron! You know what that car is worth?"

"One hundred grand?" the older man guessed.

Way more than that. Ash winced, thinking again of the money she could have made selling the car, instead of writing it off.

"Two *million*," the young guy said.

"You're kidding," said the woman.

"Seriously. This is an absolute beast of a car."

More clicks, more shuffling.

A new voice spoke up. Male. Cynical, authoritative tone. "There was someone in the car when it crashed."

There was a pause. "How do you figure that, detective?" the older man said.

"Engine still running," the detective said. "The car was built strong, the cabin especially. Therefore, just because no one's in it now doesn't mean it was empty when it hit the window."

Ash gritted her teeth. The last thing she needed right now was a smart cop.

More shuffling. "Nothing attached to the pedals," he continued. "No brick in the cabin. Someone had their foot on the accelerator."

"The driver could have jumped out before the car went over the edge of the HBS roof," the woman suggested.

"No," the detective said. "See the broken glass? How it's sprinkled all over the underside of the car? There's tonnes of it. But not a single shard is resting on any of the tyres. They were still spinning when the car stopped moving. They would have stopped in mid-air if the driver was no longer in the vehicle."

More camera clicks.

"You may also notice that the rear tyres are flat," the detective said.

"A blow-out on impact?" said the young guy.

"You saw the crash," the detective said. "The car's roof hit the window first, and now it's upside down. Unless someone's moved it, and the glass suggests they haven't, the tyres never touched the ground, or the window, or anything else in this room."

"So you think they were flat when the car left the roof?" the young guy said. "You think they contributed to the accident?"

"Take a close look at the punctures," the detective said.

Lots of shuffling. Ash listened carefully.

"What the hell?" the old guy said.

The woman: "Bullet holes."

"Here's what happened," the detective said. "Someone was shooting at this car before it went off the roof. Maybe that caused it to go off the roof. The driver survived the crash, apparently unhurt; he or she was strong enough to push out the passenger door, and there's no sign of blood anywhere. The quarantine zone has given us an advantage. Both the shooter and the driver are contained inside it. But I'm willing to bet that the driver is still in the building, so I suggest we start looking."

Ash could hardly hear him over the blood pounding in her ears.

"Mills, Baxter, you go down to the bottom floor and work your way up. Search one level at a time. Caswell, start searching this floor and work your way down. Check every room of every apartment. Check every bathroom, every cupboard, every manhole."

Ash pressed her ear against the door. She heard his next sentence very clearly. "And don't anybody touch the inside of the car," the detective said. "We'll be able to get the driver's prints off the keys."

Peachey opened the stairwell door. At least that was the problem of the girl solved. He hadn't had the satisfaction of killing her himself, but he wasn't a greedy man. And it almost counted – he'd been the one who chased her up to the roof, and who shot out her tyres. But he was reasonably confident she would have died anyhow. What was she thinking, trying a stunt like that?

Back to the plan. Hide in Buckland's office. Wait for him to come back. Kill him. Walk out.

His phone rang. That'll be Walker, he thought. Haven't heard from her in a while. He answered it. "Hel—"

"What the hell is going on?" Walker screamed.

"Hi," Peachey said.

"We are paying you for a simple task. Kill Hammond Buckland. Instead, you've broken one of Buckland's windows, thrown a member of his cleaning staff to his death, and shot at a car as it drove off the roof. You now have the attention of a live television audience, and the TRA seems to have showed up for some reason. Want to tell me what's going on?"

How did she know I was on the roof? wondered Peachey. "I'm doing my job."

"Oh, that's a relief. Because from here it looks like you're just making a mess."

Peachey pushed open the stairwell door on floor 25 and started walking towards Buckland's office. "Everything I've done has been essential to my mission," he said. "I'm setting up a trap for Buckland, and he will come to me. When he does, I'll kill him. But until then, I'd appreciate it if you'd stop calling me. When the job is done, *I* will call *you*. Got it?"

"You now have a time limit," Walker said. "You have until I find a better assassin. I'm trying to track down Alex de Totth as we speak."

"Good luck. I'm pretty sure she's dead."

"Jeremy Quay, then."

Peachey smiled. "I will complete my mission, and when I do, I expect to be paid in full." He hung up.

That was some pretty incriminating stuff. He played back the recording on the phone. *"Hel— What the hell is going on? Hi. We are paying you for a simple task. Kill Hammond Buckland."* Excellent, loud and clear. He snapped the handset shut.

He might just get paid after all.

He slowed down as he approached Buckland's office. There were people in hazard suits standing around the doorway. Their hoods were down and their masks were off.

As he raised his weapon, the leader turned to look at him. She fixed him with a moonless gaze, and her lips drew back in a hollow, perfect smile.

It was Alex de Totth.

Number one.

A red dot raced across the floor towards Peachey as she raised her pistol; a laser-fitted Browning 9 mm. Peachey jumped right, back around the corner, back the way he'd come. Even as he turned to run, even as he heard them start to move towards him, a projectile whizzed past his twisting torso, burying itself in the wall of the corridor. Someone was already shooting at him – not de Totth, though, or he'd be dead already. He broke into a sprint back down the corridor, more frightened than he'd been in a long time.

These people aren't TRA! he thought. They're assassins! It's de Totth and her team, back after six months of silence!

Whizz, thunk. Another shot at him, another miss. But barely. The sleeve of his shirt was torn above the elbow.

He couldn't outfight the world's toughest hit woman. She would end his life without a second thought. But maybe, just maybe, he could run somewhere she wouldn't find him.

The lift was up ahead. No good. He'd have to wait for it to arrive, and it would only take a moment of standing still before he looked like a used target sheet.

His best chance was the stairwell. They clearly wanted something in Buckland's office, so they wouldn't follow him too far away from it. He crashed through the stairwell door, wincing as he heard the *crack-crack* of more gunshots behind him, and slammed it closed.

He didn't bother with the stairs. He was more scared of de Totth than of potentially plunging twenty-five storeys to his death. He vaulted over the banister, and was already falling as he heard the hazard-suited guys burst through the door behind him.

He fell three storeys before grabbing a banister. He gasped as his torso smashed against the landing, and he thought he heard a crack from his ribs, but he held on. He stared upwards. Were they following?

No movement up above. Maybe he was okay. Maybe they wouldn't—

De Totth peered over the railing on the top floor, almost curiously. She looked down at him, dangling twenty-two storeys above certain oblivion. She cocked her Browning, and Peachey watched the red dot creep across the concrete.

He couldn't drag himself up. He couldn't let go. There was nothing he could do.

He watched her inky black eyes examine the situation. Watched her wonder if the unusual shot was worth risking her "never miss" reputation for.

Then she holstered her gun and walked away. Out of view.

Peachey dangled there for a moment. He was confused. This mission was like a nightmare, and made about as much sense – and it just kept getting worse.

What was de Totth doing here, on today of all days? Why did she think hazard suits were a good disguise? What did they want with Buckland's office? And why hadn't she killed him, her nearest rival? If their roles had been reversed, he would have opened fire and kept pulling the trigger until he heard the splat of her hitting the ground or he ran out of bullets, whichever came first.

He tried to pull himself up over the railing, but he was exhausted and his chest was in agony. He considered dropping down a level, but wasn't yet confident he'd be able to do it without slipping and falling.

For the moment he was stuck here. This wasn't as big a problem as it would have been ten minutes ago, when Alex de Totth was pursuing him.

They called her "the Heartbreaker". And it was an unpleasantly literal title. She was said to be able to put a 9 mm slug through a human heart at a range of 50 metres,

100 per cent of the time – and that was with an ordinary pistol. She was a legend.

And now Peachey had her on his trail.

He was in an impossible position. If he left without killing Buckland, the government would try to kill him. Even the incriminating recording might not be enough to save him if he didn't complete the job. But if he stayed and tried to find Buckland, de Totth would kill him. Her team had opened fire the moment they saw him, which meant that he was on their hit list.

This sucks, he thought.

He finally dragged himself up onto the landing, and sat in the corner. It seemed as good a place as any to hide while he contemplated how well and truly screwed he was. At least no one could sneak up on him. Maybe Buckland would happen to use the stairs, Peachey could kill him and his problems would be solved.

Still. While I know de Totth is here to kill me, Peachey thought, I also know she has another purpose. If she didn't, I'd be dead already. She would have come down the steps as I was hanging from the railing, pressed her pistol against my forehead and blown me away.

She hadn't. Therefore, there was something more urgent. Something in Buckland's office that required her immediate attention, perhaps – she and her team had made a beeline for it. What were they doing? Looking for someone? Looking for something?

Peachey frowned. He remembered the girl, the student, and how she'd tapped on the walls and moved the furniture around in Buckland's office. Had she planted something for de Totth to find? Or had she been searching for the same thing de Totth was now looking for?

I should have asked her, Peachey thought. Before chasing her off the roof.

New thought. Who had hired de Totth?

Walker had said she was *looking* for de Totth, not that she had already hired her to take out Peachey. Had that been deliberate misdirection on her part, or was she uninvolved in this?

If there really was something valuable hidden in Buckland's office, then maybe de Totth was working to her own plan. It wasn't unheard of for assassins to make up their own jobs from time to time. And while employers sometimes tried to terminate their hitters to distance themselves, keep secrets or save money, the hitters often killed their employers for the same reasons.

Ordinarily, if someone was trying to kill Peachey, he'd just take them out first. Pre-emptive strike. Nine times out of ten, the one who makes the first move wins any conflict. This rule applies for assassins, gang warfare, bar fights, chess – even noughts and crosses. And if he knew where the person was, in this case in Buckland's office, he would move towards it as quickly and invisibly as he could. Then, if the person was there, he would kill them, and if they weren't, he'd hide until they showed up.

But this wasn't an ordinary situation. This was the Heartbreaker. The one person in the entire world Michael Peachey was legitimately afraid of. He couldn't outsmart her, he couldn't outrun her, he couldn't outfight her and he couldn't sneak up on her. There was nothing to do except get as far away from her as possible and hope that something distracted her before she came after him.

But if he did that, the government would hunt him down and kill him. Back to square one.

Goddamn it! He punched the wall, his Kevlar gloves smacking against the stone. What the hell do I do now?

There was a thump from down below. Peachey listened carefully. There was more than one stairwell in the building, and as far as he knew the lifts were still working. Therefore, just because he'd last seen de Totth a few floors above him didn't mean she was still up there. But if she and her team were trying to sneak up on him from below, they wouldn't be making thumping noises.

He peered over the edge of the landing. He couldn't see anything, but he heard the distant clacking of shoes against concrete. Someone was down there. Sounded like just the one person.

Peachey hadn't seen any civilians in a while – he was under the impression that everyone had been evacuated or confined to their offices or something. Probably under orders from the phoney TRA officers. So if someone was out and about, and it wasn't one of de Totth's comrades, then it was probably Hammond Buckland.

Peachey pulled out the Beretta as he rose to his feet without a sound. Completing his mission, and quickly, seemed to be his one chance of getting out of this mess alive. Up to now, he had wanted to kill Buckland for the money. For the prestige. For the revenge. But not any more.

Now, he thought, it's him or me.

He crept down the stairs.

PART THREE

Evasive Manoeuvres

Detective Wright paced the corridors. He'd given his team set paths to follow in their search for the driver of the car, but he liked to go his own way. He tried to picture the apartments as the driver would have seen them, putting himself in the man or woman's situation.

If I'd just driven a two million dollar car through the window of a hundred grand per year apartment, he asked himself, where would I be?

The walking felt too random. If he found anything this way, it would be by accident. He returned to the ruined apartment and stood in the doorway, looking out.

Okay. I've just stumbled out of the wreckage. I'm unhurt, but presumably dazed. I don't want to be trapped.

I head towards the lifts.

Wright started walking again. But I don't take the lifts, he thought. There was no one on their way down when we were on our way up. Why? And where do I go instead?

I'm scared, he thought. I've been shot at, I've been in a car crash. And I think someone's still after me. So when I see that the lift is coming up, my first reaction is to turn and run.

So. Three possibilities to add to the profile of the driver. One: I've been unconscious, and I don't know for how long, so I think it's plausible that the shooter from the HBS roof is already here. Two: the shooter is part of a group who are out to get me, so my instinct is to avoid everyone. Three: I'm irrational, either because of a head wound from the crash or a pre-existing condition.

Wright started walking away from the lifts, hurrying like the driver probably had. I'd be looking for another way down, he thought. Another lift, or a stairwell. But the lift takes, what? Fifteen seconds to get from the ground floor to here with no stops? So I don't have long. Which means I either sprint down to the end of this corridor – it's possible – or I duck into one of these other apartments.

Wright braced himself to kick open the door. Then he

stopped. The chances of the driver having a key card to one of these apartments was practically zero. And the likelihood of him or her being able to hack the lock in under fifteen seconds and with no tools was negligible. The locks hadn't been broken, either; therefore the driver wasn't in any of the apartments.

"This is Wright," he said into his radio. "I'm revising your orders. No need to check any apartment that has been electronically locked."

"Couldn't the driver have locked them from the inside?" Caswell crackled.

"Not without getting inside first," Wright said. "These doors close themselves, and the locks engage automatically." He smiled. This would narrow their search considerably.

Wright's eyes were drawn to the janitor's closet door. It had no lock. It was large enough to fit a person, but small enough to make a good hiding place. Far enough away from the lifts to feel safe, but close enough to stumble inside within the fifteen-second margin.

Wright pressed his ear against the door. No sound inside.

He stepped back. Took a deep breath. Then charged, shoulder-first, against the door.

It snapped open, and Wright stepped back immediately, just in case someone jumped out at him.

No one did.

The closet was empty.

Wright stepped inside, just to be sure. He'd seen suspects conceal themselves in smaller spaces than this. But there was no one hidden behind the buckets. No one lying on shelves above. No one behind the door.

Disappointed but determined, he closed the door and kept pacing.

Ash didn't dare poke her head out the door to see how far away the detective was. By listening, she could tell that he was over by the janitor's closet, but she couldn't tell which way he was facing. If he was turned towards the lifts, and she peeped out the door of the apartment she was in, he would see her. And she'd be busted.

Ash was in the apartment the police had broken into while searching for the car. When she'd been inside the janitor's closet and had heard their footsteps march towards the lifts, she had opened the closet door a crack, planning to run and find a better hiding place. But she hadn't been able to leave; one guy, who she assumed was the detective, was still in the destroyed apartment. He was staring thoughtfully at the wreckage, shifting his weight from one foot to the other.

Ash had waited. After a long, tense minute, the detective had left the apartment and started walking along the corridor.

He followed his team towards the lifts, and Ash, knowing that at least two of the cops had been instructed to search this floor and would therefore be back soon, had fled from the closet.

She had moved towards the apartment with the car in it. She needed to steal the keys so they couldn't be tested for fingerprints. She had never been printed, so her prints couldn't lead the police directly to her, and as far as she knew her prints had never been found at any of her other jobs. So there wasn't much risk of her getting caught right away. But if the cops got her fingerprints from the keys, and she was ever fingerprinted in the future – whether it was for a job interview or after an arrest – she would be instantly linked to the Veyron. And she had no idea how she could convincingly talk her way out of that situation.

Of course, Ash knew that there was very little chance of her living long enough to have a job interview or get arrested. From what Benjamin had told her about anthrax, she was as good as dead. But there was a slim possibility that she would make it out of this building, be able to break into the TRA truck, and find the drugs she needed to survive. She had to cling to that chance. And if things worked out that way, she didn't want to go to jail. So she needed those keys.

When she had arrived in the doorway of the crash-site apartment, she had discovered that a photographer was still in there. He had been facing away from her, so she'd been able to duck back outside without being spotted. But now she was in the middle of the corridor, in plain view. Exposed. And the search team would return at any moment. She could actually see the back of the detective as he studied the lift.

Thinking quickly, Ash had ducked through the other doorway the cops had broken open. With any luck, their search would not include locked rooms they had opened themselves. She was still there now, back pressed against the wall, listening for any movement outside.

Standing in this apartment was slightly surreal, because it looked exactly as the other one must have before the Veyron plunged through the window. Luxuriously furnished, with a plump four-poster bed and a crisp television. The table in the kitchen was cold and black. The light fittings on the walls looked like smooth plastic ice-cream cones with light melting down the sides.

Although she knew it made no sense, she kept glancing out the window, expecting a car to fly in through it. Like she'd somehow travelled back in time, and was standing in the ruined apartment right before she'd ruined it.

She wished she could close the door – she felt so vulnerable with it open. But the police had kicked it open, jamming the automatic closing mechanism. They would become suspicious if they saw it had shut itself. Particularly the detective. He was smart. Way smarter than Ash was comfortable with.

She heard the detective close the janitor's closet door. Then he started coming back her way.

Ash retreated into the bedroom of the apartment, willing him not to come any closer.

His footsteps grew louder. A muffled, careful metronome.

Ash pulled the sheets on the bed to one side so that the edge hung to the floor on the side nearest the window. She lay down between the bed and the sofa, took a deep breath, and held it.

She heard the faded rustle of carpet depressed by a shoe. Then nothing. Then the rustle again.

The detective was in the apartment.

The bathroom door creaked open. Ash prayed he would step inside, so she could sneak out past him. Then she could hide in the janitor's closet again. No way would he check in there twice.

But no. He had opened the door, but wasn't walking through it. He hadn't even switched on the light.

He knows I'm here, Ash thought, hairs rising on the back of her neck. He *wants* me to make a break for it.

The detective stepped towards the bed. Ash heard his knees crack as he crouched to look under it. The sheet she had pulled aside was screening her from his view. Her vision was glittering from the lack of oxygen. Her lungs felt like they were filled with tennis balls.

The detective stood up. Ash slowly and silently rolled underneath the bed, pushing the sheet aside with care, then letting it hang back where it had been. The detective walked around to the other side of the bed. Ash imagined him staring at the space she had occupied a moment ago.

There was a grinding sound as he pushed the couch aside, apparently checking if anyone was behind it. Ash crept out from under the other side of the bed. She crawled slowly across the floor, resisting the temptation to turn around and see if the detective had seen her, and slipped through the open bathroom door. Her heart was pounding.

Ash slipped into the shower cubicle and shut the door. The glass was blurred and the tiles were dark, so she curled up on the floor. She figured she wouldn't be seen unless the door was opened.

The shower had recently been cleaned. It had an indoor swimming pool kind of scent.

Wright pushed the couch back into place. No one had been behind it. He had found no evidence whatsoever that there was anything out of the ordinary in this apartment. No one under the bed. No one behind the door. None of the usual places.

He opened the closet. It was a woman's apartment. Shoes that looked like miniature tangled-up power boards, jackets the size of handkerchiefs. A few narrow grey suits. He thought he smelled lavender. No one behind the coat rack, no one under the stack of winter garments. He stepped back out and closed the door.

There was no sign that anyone was in here other than him. Nothing was keeping him here other than the fact that if he was hiding, this is where he would be. He would have hidden in the janitor's closet when he saw the lift was coming. He would have doubled back to this apartment when he heard the floor was being searched, in the hope that it was the one place that wouldn't be checked.

Wright approached the bathroom door. He hadn't really looked in there before; he had listened, but then decided that he should check under the bed first. If he had entered the bathroom while there were still unexplored places in the bedroom, the driver could have left the apartment while his back was turned.

He stepped into the bathroom and clicked on the light. Cream tiles, a big mirror surrounded by light bulbs. Tiny soaps scattered around the bath as if a giant block of soap had shattered when someone threw it into the tub. A mop propped against the wall – someone had been cleaning recently, unless it belonged there. If it did, that meant the occupant lived alone. Exposed cleaning items were the hallmark of a solitary life.

The shower door was closed, and not quite transparent. Wright pulled it open.

There was a scream from inside, and he stepped back, astonished. A teenage girl was cowering in the corner, looking up at him through a cage of fingers. She was wearing a white blouse, blue jeans and a jacket – neither having a shower nor cleaning it. Tears were dribbling from her pine-needle coloured eyes.

"Please don't kill me," she said.

Wright reached into his jacket for his badge. She whimpered and pressed herself against the wall.

"My name is Damien Wright," he said. "I'm a policeman." He held up his badge, but she was trembling as if she was trying to melt and escape down the drain.

"Please," she said again.

"I'm not going to hurt you," he said. "What's your name?"

"Ash," she said. "Ash Redgrave." She sniffed. "I live here with my mum."

Wright held out his hand to help her up. She ignored it, staring at him with suspicion.

"Are you really a policeman?" she asked.

"A detective," Wright said. "You want to tell me what you're doing here?"

"I live here," she said. "I already said that."

"I meant in the shower."

After a moment, she took his hand and stood up. Her fingers were cold.

"I heard a noise," she said. "Like a thunderclap, or an explosion. I could feel it through the wall. And I got scared, so I listened for a while, but I couldn't hear anything. So I went to the window—"

"Why wasn't your mother home?"

"She left a couple of hours ago; she works nights. Then someone broke down my door, so I ducked behind the bed, and then I heard people talking and moving, and then they broke down another door outside and then I hid in the bathroom..."

Wright led her out into the bedroom again. She stood by the bed and tugged at the sheets, straightening them. She looked nervous, confused. A hint of uncertainty. Exactly what you'd expect from a girl who'd had to hide in her bathroom while her door was broken down by police.

"Why are there people outside?" she asked. "In the street, with the roadblocks and stuff? Was that noise...you know, an explosion? Like a terrorist attack?"

Exactly what you'd expect her to assume.

Wright lunged forwards and shoved her against the wall. She yelped – not fear, but surprise. She tried to step aside as he kept coming, but he slammed a hand against the wall, trapping her between him and the bedpost. He put his forearm against her chest and held her in place.

"You're lying to me," he said.

She looked uncomprehending and confused.

"You don't live here," he said. "One bed, one bathroom. Expensive suits in the closet. Your mum's rich, but she makes you sleep on the couch instead of buying a bed? You don't go outside to investigate when there's an explosion next door? You don't close the door when it's kicked down? No. Only one person belongs in this apartment, and it isn't you."

To her credit, the girl kept it up. She struggled against his arm, staring at him like he was crazy. He almost doubted himself.

"You don't live here," he continued. "Redgrave isn't your real name. You drove a Bugatti Veyron off the roof of HBS because you were being shot at. You landed in the apartment next door. You climbed out and went to the lifts, but we were already on our way up, so you hid in the janitor's closet. Then you waited for us to leave the crime scene. When we started searching for you, you doubled back and came in here, hoping we wouldn't find you. And now that I have, you're going to tell me everything. You know why?"

The girl said nothing.

"Because you lied to me. And because you were so good

at it. That means there was no legitimate reason for you to be on that roof with that car. That means you're up to your neck in this. It means that your only chance is to cooperate with me. Then you might get immunity when your testimony indicts someone in deeper than you."

He stepped back, releasing her. She looked at him for a long moment. Then she sat down on the bed.

Wright folded his arms. Spill it, he thought. Come on. Tell me what's going on.

"Ash *is* my real name," she said finally. "And I'm the last person you should be worried about."

Peachey was in a service corridor, following Buckland, and gradually gaining on him. There was a cafeteria for employees on the second floor, and a large chunk of the same floor was taken up by the kitchens – a sprawling maze of black and white ceramic walls, steel benches, neon energy-saver bulbs. Gnarled plastic utensils dangled from hooks on every wall, and leafy ingredients overflowed from every fridge. Woven through the mess of fryers and ovens and hotplates and sinks there was a network of narrow corridors, designed to enable the service staff to move quickly and invisibly around the floor.

Why Buckland was down here, Peachey had no idea. But

this was too good an opportunity to miss. The whole place was deserted. De Totth was on the top floor. Peachey was armed; he still had half a clip in his Beretta. As soon as he got close enough to Buckland, he could put three bullets in him, torso left, torso right, skull, then get the hell out of here and go home.

Buckland turned left. Peachey turned left. Buckland turned right. Peachey turned right.

Peachey was almost within range now. But he wanted no mistakes. He'd worked too hard today to screw up now. He wanted to take the shot from close up, standing still, with Buckland walking down a long and straight stretch of corridor so there was no chance he would miss. He wasn't like Alex de Totth – his aim was good, but it wasn't superhuman.

Peachey found himself wondering why exactly the government wanted Buckland dead. Roughly six out of every ten jobs he took were for OCGs – organized crime groups, either gangs or corporations – who needed a witness taken care of before a trial. Another two would be for private citizens who stood to inherit something in a will. Another one would be for people who wanted revenge for one thing or another. Peachey liked those – they were often exciting and challenging, because the client usually wanted the mark to die in a certain way. And the last one would be the government, who invariably needed a secret kept. These jobs were either really easy or really hard, depending on whether or not the person knew the value of their information.

Peachey couldn't imagine Buckland knowing anything that could damage the government. He had never worked for, with or against them. None of his products had anything to do with defence or immigration, which were the hot topics at the moment.

And it was something important, that was for sure. Walker had offered Peachey a huge sum to do the job. Peachey normally charged a third of the value of the victim's life insurance. That wasn't a policy, it was just the way things usually worked out. If the victim was insured for $1 million, then his life was worth $333,333.33 to Peachey. Plus expenses, of course – including weaponry, surveillance equipment, travel and accommodation. And meals. No one ever complained when he presented a receipt for the shellfish, wine and tiramisu he'd consumed at the hotel. Not after they'd seen how casually he ended the lives of the people in his way.

Without breaking stride, Buckland picked up a mop that had been leaning against the wall and rounded a corner into one of the kitchens. Peachey frowned. What the hell was he up to now? He tightened his grip on the gun and kept moving. If Buckland was nearing the end of his mysterious journey, Peachey might not have much time to catch up to him and get a clear shot.

Peachey rounded the corner into the kitchen. He had time to take in the rows of oil vats and draining trays and hotplates before losing his footing and slipping over. He threw his hands back to try and break his fall and land in a crab-like crouch, but they slid out from under him as they touched the same greasy substance he'd stepped in. He saw Buckland standing over him, holding a mop that was still dripping oil onto the ground. Peachey raised his pistol.

Buckland brought the handle of the mop down on Peachey's skull with a sharp *crack*, and Peachey felt like his eyeballs were going to burst. He held his arms above his head, warding off a second blow, but Buckland slammed the mop handle into his abdomen instead, point first. Peachey gasped as the air was forced out of him. He couldn't see, or breathe, or hear. Two of his five senses were gone, and his body wasn't responding to the commands of his brain. Defying his assassin's instinct to fire only when he had a clear shot, he pulled the trigger of the Beretta, firing a few shots into the ceiling, hoping to hit Buckland.

Something hit his face, either the mop handle or a fist, and then he was lifted up into the air and dropped.

Sploonk. The sound he made as he plunged into the oil vat was like a foot into a bowl of jelly. The cold, greasy substance flooded into his nose, his eyes, and his open wheezing mouth. It writhed up his arms and legs, pushing under his shirt-cuffs and down his collar. He coughed into the oil, and more flooded into his lungs to fill the vacuum. He thrashed around, trying to rise, trying to figure out which wall was the floor so he could jump up out of the vat. His head broke the surface of the oil, and he tried to stand.

Fireworks of pain sparked across his skull as it clanked against something above him. Peachey slipped and fell back into the slimy goop, sitting neck deep in it. Buckland had put the lid on the vat, he realized. Over the dull splashing his arms made as he reached up to try and push the lid up, he heard the crunch of a lock engaging above him.

Peachey screamed, a long, desperate roar of panic. Oil flooded down his face, drizzling down from his nose and chin. He slammed his feet against the walls of the vat until he thought his ankles would break. The noise reverberated around the darkness of the chamber. There was no room to build momentum. The vat was too solid.

Click. Click. Clack. Beep.

Peachey tried to stop his breathing and listen. The oil lapped at the steel walls and tickled under his chin. What the hell was that?

A humming came from below, and Peachey's butt suddenly started to get uncomfortably hot. He screamed louder than before once he realized what had happened.

Buckland had switched on the frying mechanism under the oil vat.

Peachey threw his fists against the lid above his head. His knuckles broke against the steel, not even rattling it. He crouched, getting as much of his body out of the oil as he could, pressing his back against the lid. The soles of his feet were on fire, even through his shoes. The skin of his shins stung, and his face burned as the air temperature in the confined space rose.

Most deep fryers heat up to roughly 290 degrees Celsius. Enough to vaporize 60 per cent of Peachey's body. Enough to turn his hair into charcoal. Enough to cook his skin into a hard brown seal that would splinter apart as his blood boiled beneath it.

The oil didn't bubble, but Peachey heard a horrible hissing from everywhere it was touching his flesh. He braced his feet against the floor and shoved against the lid, but now the metal singed his fingers. The air fried his chest from the inside. He kept his eyes squeezed shut. His nostrils felt like they were filling up with acid.

Crunch. Clank.

The lid opened above him, and light poured into the vat. Peachey wiped the grease out of his eyes with the back of his greasy gun hand, and stared up. The golden glow of the oil illuminated Alex de Totth's face as she stared down at Peachey.

He tried to rise to his feet, but she shoved him back. He splashed back down into the oil.

I'll kill you, he screamed inside his brain. I'll kill—

De Totth raised her gun, pointed it at his heart, and pulled the trigger.

Peachey barely heard the shot before the world was sucked away, like a TV screen someone had switched off.

"You don't know his name?"

Ash shook her head. She had told him the whole story, with two little exceptions. One, she had left out the part where she was a thief – she had told Wright that she was at HBS as part of a high school work-experience programme. And two, she hadn't told him about the anthrax. She figured she'd have better luck breaking into the TRA truck than sitting around in a quarantine waiting to die.

She was going to have to play this delicately. Wright was smart. She needed to convince him that her crimes were minor compared to those of the guy who'd shot at her on the HBS roof, so Wright would go after him instead of her. But she couldn't imply that she knew too much, or she'd immediately be taken into custody as a witness. And she had to talk him into letting her go quickly, before it was too late to get the anti-anthrax medication from the TRA van.

"All I know for sure is that he's a guy with a gun who tried to kill me," she said. "I didn't stick around to find out who he was or why. I just jumped in an unlocked car and drove."

"A car that was parked on the roof," Wright said doubtfully.

"It's not my business where Mr. Buckland keeps his car, or why."

"With the keys in it."

"Well, why would there be car thieves on the roof?" Ash said.

"Back to the shooter. Did he say anything to you?"

"No. At first I thought he was a thief, but now I think it's something much worse."

"It *is* much worse," Wright said. "If you're telling the truth, he was probably the guy who killed the window cleaner we found in the dumpster this morning. What I need to find out is why."

"I've got a theory about that," Ash said. "Means to an end. And even if I tell you my theory, there's nothing you can do about it."

"Yes I can. I'm with the police. We can arrest him."

"No you can't. He's protected."

"By who?" Wright demanded.

"His employers."

"I can arrest them too."

"No you can't," Ash said. "I think they're the government."

Wright frowned. "That doesn't make any sense," he said.

"Buckland told me that the government was trying to stop him from spending his money because they planned to inherit it once he died. He also said he was leaving the country tomorrow to get out from under their control. I don't think the guy was a thief at all. I think he was a hit man working for the government, who wanted Buckland killed before he had a chance to leave."

"That doesn't explain the terrorist threat inside the building, and the TRA showing up."

"Yes it does," Ash said. "I saw the hit man go into Buckland's office at 5 p.m., and Buckland was definitely inside. But an hour later I saw Buckland wandering around the corridors of floor 23. Therefore, the first attempt was aborted or unsuccessful. The government decides their assassin needs backup, so they send in the TRA – the one department that answers to no one, under the guise of national security. The threat was faked as an excuse to get more government agents inside that building, all with the job of killing Hammond Buckland."

An explosion of coughs rattled her chest. Her nose was running again.

She hoped her version of the story would make sense to

him. Because as far as she could tell, the truth made no sense at all.

"It still doesn't add up," Wright said, leaning forward confidentially. "And I'll tell you why. The body we found in the dumpster? It belonged to a federal agent."

Ash gaped. What?

"Why would a government assassin kill a government agent on the scene?" Wright continued. "Why would the agent even be there?"

"For surveillance," Ash guessed, desperate. "They were monitoring Buckland undercover in the weeks leading up to the job. When the hit man arrived, maybe he didn't know they were on his side."

"I think it's much more likely," Wright said, "that the terrorist threat is real, and that the guy who shot at you is working with the terrorists. Which leads me back to the question of who you really are and what you were really doing at HBS in the first place."

If she mentioned the essay competition, he would find out her real name. Instead, Ash said, "I want a lawyer."

Wright shrugged and stood up. "Fine."

Ash started to rise, but Wright pushed her back down against the bed. He forced her wrist against the bedpost, and snicked his handcuffs around it. "I'm arresting you for suspicion of grand theft auto and destruction of property," he said. "You do not have to say anything, but it may harm your defence if you do not mention, when questioned, something which you later rely on in court. Anything you do say may be given in evidence."

He walked towards the door. "I'll take you to the station once the quarantine is lifted," he said without turning around. "There'll be a lawyer there." And he closed the door behind him.

Ash immediately stood up and slid her hands down the bedpost behind her back. She twisted her hips so she could reach the back pocket of her jeans, and pulled out her iPod headphones. Then she climbed onto the bed and lay down so she could put them in her ears without taking her hands away from the bedpost.

"Benjamin?" she said.

"Still here, Ash," he said. "I take it you're in a bit of trouble."

"I'm under arrest, handcuffed to a bed, infected with anthrax, and I might have only minutes before that detective comes back."

"Could be worse, then."

"You bet," Ash said. "I'm not injured, not currently under guard, and they don't know my real name. And I still have my iPod." She smiled as she kicked off her left shoe. "I still have you."

Benjamin didn't reply.

"Are the roadblocks still up?" she asked quickly.

"Uh, yeah," Benjamin said. "A news helicopter has flown in for live footage, and it's parked on top of the apartment building, so I can see everything. I guess this means it'll take a while for Wright to get you out of there."

"I was hoping you'd say that," Ash said, picking up the shoe. Handcuffs are much more difficult to pick in real life than in the movies. The ones with a metal block instead of a chain are almost impossible, because they hold your wrists together, keeping your fingers away from the key slot. Fortunately, most handcuff keys in the world are exactly the same. Any one of these universal keys will open almost any pair of handcuffs. And Ash had one sealed in the left sole of every pair of shoes she owned. Now she just had to get it open.

"Is the TRA van still outside?" she asked.

"Yes. The antibiotics you need are penicillin, doxycycline, and…wait. Oh my god!"

"What?" Ash demanded, alarmed. "What's going on?"

"You're not going to die!" Benjamin blurted out.

"What?" Ash's heart beat faster. "How come? What have you found?"

"The anthrax was fake!" Benjamin said. "I wasn't quite certain of the picture, so I did a full chemical analysis of the sample data you sent me. It just finished compiling. It's not really anthrax, it's baby powder or something!"

"Are you sure?" Ash demanded. "You're not making this up, or guessing, or hoping? You know for certain?"

"I know for certain, babe. You're going to be fine!"

"But I've had the flu symptoms you warned me about," she said. "Coughing fits. A runny nose. A headache. If I haven't had anthrax, what's wrong with me?"

"Best guess?" Benjamin said. "I'd say you've got the flu."

Ash exhaled, emptying her lungs completely, like she was finally expelling the last of that breath Benjamin had asked her to hold when she first opened the box. She laughed quietly until tears were flooding down her cheeks. She punched the bed with her free hand and stamped her feet and smiled until her face hurt. Then, once she'd wiped her face and regulated her breathing and her heart rate was down to normal, she picked up the shoe and resumed her attempts to open the sole.

"You know what this means?"

"We should have a candlelit dinner at a fancy restaurant to celebrate," Benjamin said instantly.

"Nope," Ash said. The compartment in the sole opened, and the handcuff key popped out. "It means it's time to get back to work. We have $200 million to steal."

Life After Death

Peachey opened his eyes.

His burned eyelids stung as they scrunched up above his eyeballs. The world was a gluey blur – he was still drenched in oil. He tried to move, and his limbs barely responded, squidging inch by inch across the tiles.

But he was thinking, feeling. His heart still beat in his chest. His fried lungs still sucked in air.

He was alive. Against all odds, he was alive.

He groaned, a long, rattling sound. The last thing he remembered was Alex de Totth firing a gun into his heart at point-blank range as he was drowning in a vat of boiling oil. What the hell had happened? Was he dead? Because, frankly, he'd hoped the afterlife would be less slippery.

He lifted his right arm off the ground, and it hurt like hell – like there were weights strapped to the joints. He endured the pain and wiped the oil out of his eyes with his hand. Then he raised his head to look at his body.

He actually looked okay. His suit was beyond ruined, of course, but his skin was pink and raw rather than crystallized into charcoal as he'd expected. He tried to find the bullet wound in his chest. Had de Totth, for the first time in her career, missed the heart of her victim?

Peachey frowned. There was something sticking out of his chest. He tugged it out and stared at it.

It was a tranquillizer dart.

De Totth and her team weren't using live ammunition. They hadn't planned to kill him at all. Then what the hell were they doing?

Peachey clambered to his feet. He was still in the kitchen, and there was a hose looped against the kitchen wall. He staggered over to it, picked up the nozzle, pointed it at his head, and twisted the tap.

Water blasted across his face, cleaving through the oil like a windscreen wiper through rain. He lowered his head so the spray could cleanse his hair. The water was deliciously cold as it trickled down his collar. He opened his mouth to catch some, swilled it around his oil-stained teeth, and spat it out.

He rinsed his torso, his arms and his hands, and his legs and his feet. Pretty soon he was completely soaked, and felt almost human again. He tossed the hose to the floor and switched it off.

It disturbed him how little he understood the situation. Why did de Totth want to keep him alive? He was her nearest rival. He wanted to kill her. So why stick him with a tranquillizer dart and leave him in the kitchen? Is this a game to her? he wondered.

Maybe she wanted the bounty on Buckland. She'd knocked Peachey out to get him out of the picture, then contacted Walker and gone billionaire-hunting.

But that didn't make sense. She could have left him in the deep fryer if that were the case.

Peachey couldn't find his Beretta. Not in his pockets, not in the oil vat, not on the floor under any of the benches. De Totth must have taken it. That was two guns lost in one day.

Maybe disarming him had been her objective. But why keep him alive?

Maybe it was Buckland who'd taken his gun away. Peachey couldn't remember whether he'd still had it in his hand when Buckland threw him into the vat.

Peachey screwed his eyes shut and gritted his teeth. He

wound his fingers through his hair and tugged until it hurt. Focus, he told himself.

He decided to stick with the plan. He had no other options. Go to Buckland's office, kill Buckland, leave the building. He'd do it with his bare hands if he had to. But now it wasn't just a matter of money. It had nothing to do with reputation. It wasn't about what the government would do to him if he failed his mission.

It was going to feel good, though. Buckland had made Peachey angry. Peachey wouldn't walk away even if he could.

Peachey ran back through the maze of service corridors towards the stairwell. He had one thing in his favour. By now, Buckland *must* believe Peachey was dead. He'd hit him on the head, dropped him into a deep fryer, locked the lid and switched it on. There weren't a lot of ways to survive that, and if de Totth hadn't come along, Peachey would be a lump of charcoal by now. So Buckland wouldn't be expecting another attack from him.

What's more, he'd be distracted by de Totth and her team. Whatever it was they were here to take, it was a fair bet that Buckland didn't want them to take it. So he'd be focusing on them while Peachey crept up on him from behind.

That's why de Totth saved me, he realized suddenly. She's hoping that I'll be the distraction, trying to kill Buckland while she robs him blind.

He shoved open the stairwell door. Fine. She can do her thing, I'll do mine.

"You're kidding," Benjamin said, more amused than appalled. Maybe he was still on an "Ash isn't dying" high. "After all this, you're going back in there?"

"You think after all this I'd just give up?" Ash replied. "No way." Her handcuffs clicked open, and she tiptoed to the front door. She pushed her ear against it. No one was coming, but there was someone out there, shifting their weight from foot to foot. Wright had posted a guard. Smart – but he should've put them inside the room.

"You know, not having anthrax doesn't make you invincible," Benjamin said. "You're still vulnerable to bullets, car crashes and kryptonite."

"I'm planning on avoiding those particular things." Ash went over to the window and looked out. The HBS building stood proudly above her, silhouetted by a washed-out rising moon. Car headlights sparkled in the distant streets.

"Based on your previous adventures inside HBS, they're not going to be easy to avoid. Well, except the kryptonite. And I wouldn't be surprised if the government agents brought some just for you."

"Wrong," Ash said. "The hit man thinks I'm dead, so he

and his government backup are only concerned with Buckland. There's only one more place on our list to search: the basement. I'll get in, find the money, walk out with it, and wait for the police to take down the roadblocks."

"You promise to go straight to the basement, and straight out again?" Benjamin sounded serious now. "I cannot describe how much it would suck if only hours after you were spared from death by anthrax you got killed in the crossfire between Buckland and the government."

Ash bit her lip as she pulled the duvet off the bed. Benjamin had just given her a moral dilemma to consider. Could she really steal the money and otherwise mind her own business while the government killed Hammond Buckland upstairs?

She hadn't made him rich. She hadn't made the government greedy. But still, wasn't she obligated to do something? Didn't having advance warning of the plan make her partly responsible if he died?

There wasn't a lot she could do. She was a thief, not a bodyguard – and she would be outnumbered. But still, Buckland didn't deserve to die. And the guy who'd shot at her from the roof didn't deserve to win.

Buckland was almost a stranger. She owed him nothing. She would be risking her life if she tried to save him.

But still.

"Yes," she said finally. "Straight in, straight out. I'll keep out of danger."

"Thanks, Ash."

"I'm hoping Wright will send some cops into the building anyway," Ash said. "TRA can't keep people out for ever – not without exposing what's going on." She pressed the blanket up against the window, near the wall. She dragged a chair towards her, then raised her leg and held the blanket in place against the glass. Then she lifted the chair with one arm, and bashed it against the window.

The glass was thick; it didn't break first time. But the sound was deadened enough by the blanket that Ash didn't think there was a risk of being heard by the guard outside. She swung the chair again.

Shards of glass clinked against one another under the blanket. Ash lowered her leg, now uncomfortably aware that she was at least twenty storeys above ground, and started pushing on the broken window through the duvet, widening the hole.

"How are you going to get back into HBS?" Benjamin asked.

"You'll see," Ash said. But so far, she had no idea.

She snatched the blanket away, like a magician revealing a bird from under a handkerchief. The window yawned toothily at her, and the wind ruffled her hair. She started breaking off chunks of broken glass on the left-hand side, the side closest to the wall. She kept going until she reached the frame of the window, so she could run her hands up and down the frame without getting cut. Then she went back to the bed and started twisting the sheets into a rope.

She felt absurdly teenage as she tied one end of the rope around the bedpost she had been cuffed to and the other around her belt. Just an average fifteen-year-old girl, making abseiling equipment out of bedclothes, climbing out the window because she'll be busted if she opens her door.

She shook off the image. Cops, not parents. Twenty storeys, not two. Two hundred million dollars instead of a secret boyfriend.

And she was hardly an average girl.

She stood on the edge of the floor and leaned out into the void, clutching the wall to her left. The people pressing at the roadblocks below were so far down they looked like specks of seasoning on a crisp.

The rope held. If she fell, she wouldn't die. In theory.

The rope was nowhere near long enough to get her close enough to the ground so that she could drop down safely. Instead, she was hoping she'd be able to climb into the apartment next door.

She reached out to her left, stretching her arm to its limit. The wall between her apartment and the one the Veyron had landed in was only half a metre thick, so she could reach the opposite edge. She took a long, shaky breath. Then she jumped.

Her stomach scraped against the concrete and she wrapped her arms around the wall like a cat clinging to a tree trunk. The rope billowed out behind her. She hoped that no one happened to be looking up, and that if they were, the light was sufficiently poor and her face shielded enough that no cameras would be able to make it out. This would be a lousy way to get famous.

She craned her neck to peer into the ruined apartment. The crime-scene photographers were gone. About time.

She stretched her leg out and touched the floor of the crash-site apartment with her toes. It wasn't as close as she would have liked. She reached out further, and was able to put her whole foot flat against the floor. But she couldn't just step in – she was going to have to jump.

Ash braced her leg against the wall, and counted to three in her head. Then she counted again, because she still couldn't muster up the courage the first time. Then she jumped.

Her foot scuffled against the carpet of the crash-site apartment, and for a terrifying moment she thought she was going to slip. But then her sole caught against the fibres of the floor and she managed to shove the rest of her body forwards. She almost landed on all fours before the rope jerked tight, and her hands were suspended just above the floor. She wriggled backwards a little bit to get some more slack, then reached back and untied the rope. Free, she slumped face first against the carpet, ignoring the scratches of broken glass particles against her chin.

"Benjamin," she panted, "did you see me on the news?"

"What? No. Why? What did you do?"

"Good," she said.

She tore off a piece of the curtain and used it to wipe her prints from the inside of the Bugatti Veyron. The keys were the most crucial part, obviously, but she did the steering wheel, door handles and dashboard as well. There was a single hair on the headrest, and while she knew for a fact that no one had her DNA on file, she removed it anyway. She checked the seat for fibres from her jeans, and gave everything a quick, final wipe. Then she threw the piece of curtain out the window. It danced away along the breeze.

Now her problem would be getting out of the apartment. Depending on where the guard outside the other apartment was standing, he might be able to see the door to this one. If that was the case, she'd need a diversion before leaving.

Ash walked into the kitchen. The walls must be sturdy; the car crash in the bedroom hadn't knocked a single item off the shelves in here. She opened up the liquor cabinet and took out a bottle of Bailey's Irish Cream. She popped the lid and sniffed it. Yuck. People actually drank this?

She walked back to the window frame and picked up the sheet-rope she'd used to rappel in. She poured Bailey's along it, then threw the bottle around the corner so it landed in the adjacent apartment with a crash.

"Any ideas about who would put fake anthrax in HBS?" she asked Benjamin as she walked back to the kitchen.

"Forget who would. Who *could*? You had a pretty tough time getting into that room, and you weren't carrying a coffin-sized box."

"The room obviously isn't guarded around the clock. The only reason we didn't look for the money later at night is that we don't have the resources to break in."

"So the culprit is someone who does," Benjamin said. "Terrorist groups would use real anthrax, so it's probably not them."

"Rival corporation?" Ash suggested.

"What rival corporation?" Benjamin countered. "And besides, how would they benefit from an anthrax scare? It'd barely make a dent in HBS's share price. The risks would far outweigh the benefits."

Ash took a gas lighter out of a drawer, and clicked it a couple of times to check that it worked. "So, back to my original idea. The government put it there because they thought their hit man needed backup. The fake anthrax gets found, the TRA gets called in."

"Brilliant," Benjamin said. "You're a genius."

Ash sighed as she washed her hands at the sink. She knew that tone.

"Except," Benjamin continued, "that the box must have been there since at least last night, because that's the only time a break-in could happen. And the government wouldn't have known the hitter needed backup until this morning."

"Square one," Ash said.

"Square one," Benjamin confirmed. "Still, does it matter? I mean, is it relevant?"

"It's all relevant. It's all connected. Somehow." Ash picked up the dripping sheet-rope and walked to the window frame.

"Is it relevant to our job?" Benjamin said. "Finding the money?"

"We'll find out soon," Ash said. She clicked the gas lighter under the end of the rope, and dropped it out into the void as it ignited.

The flames tore up across the rope, racing into the adjacent apartment. With any luck, the bed would catch fire, and the leftover Bailey's from the bottle would light up too. Ash ran to the door, and listened.

She didn't have long to wait. The guard apparently didn't notice the fire itself, but he heard the alarm. A piercing electronic shriek came from the other apartment, and Ash heard the guard opening the door to investigate.

Now! She ducked out of her apartment and sprinted down the hallway, away from the lifts, hoping to reach the corner before he came out again. Fifteen metres. Ten. Five.

She rounded the corner, and didn't stop. There were no shouts from behind her, but she could bet the guard had reported her missing on his radio. The fire, the rope and the broken window would confuse them at first, but it wouldn't be long before Detective Wright and his entire team were back on her trail.

They would expect her to head for the ground floor, and to try to get through the roadblock. Ash pushed open the stairwell door and started sprinting up the stairs three at a time.

She had a helicopter to catch.

Wright ran out of the lift and sprinted down the corridor like a hound after a rabbit. He burst in through the apartment door, and staggered right back out again. The apartment was already a furnace, flames crackling and spitting all over the carpet, the thunderous blaze overpowered by the screaming of the alarm. If the girl was in there she was already dead – but he was betting she wasn't in there.

He dragged Mills and Baxter back out the door and slammed it shut.

"The sprinkler system will take care of it," he said. "If the door's closed it won't spread. Baxter, take the stairs down to the ground floor and wait for the suspect to try and escape. Mills, start searching this floor with me." He eyeballed the two cops. "This is all part of her plan. So look sharp, search well, search fast and assume nothing. Got it?"

The two officers nodded and split up. Wright pressed his ear to the door. It was cold, but he could still hear the popping and snarling of the flames. Damn – he wanted to get in there and take a look so he could work out how she'd escaped.

He crouched, staring at the carpet. When I left, she was handcuffed to the bedpost. I know I put the cuffs on tight. The bedpost was welded to the frame at both ends. She didn't have any pins in her hair to pick the lock. And there was a guard standing outside the only door. Outside the only window, it's – what? An 80-metre fall to the ground?

If he was right and she truly wasn't in there, burned to a crisp, or splattered over the road outside having plummeted to her death, then it was one of the best escapes from custody he had ever seen. He'd given her nothing to work with, and she'd still escaped. He wanted to know how it had been done, and he was already formulating some ideas.

But she was his responsibility; if she got away, it was his fault. He could have cuffed all four limbs to different posts so as she couldn't move at all. He could have put a tracking collar on her.

He should have put Mills inside the room instead of outside the door.

Wright hadn't wanted the girl telling Mills her theories about government involvement in this crisis. If it was true and there was a conspiracy, just knowing about it would put Mills in danger. If it was false, Mills might lose faith in Wright for taking it seriously. That was why he'd asked Mills to stay outside.

But he doubted that was a good enough excuse. Maybe he should have gagged the girl and then put Mills inside. But it was too late now. He had to find her.

Wright stood up and started pacing the corridor, like before. Although he figured Mills would have already checked, he ripped open the janitor's closet door. No one inside. He shoved open the door to the crash-site apartment and stormed in. Empty. He kicked down the door of the next apartment, vetoing his earlier conclusion that the suspect couldn't be inside locked rooms. Pristine, untouched, deserted. He strode out again.

"Detective?" It was his radio. *"It's Elton."*

Wright held it up to his face as he kicked open the next

apartment door. "Have you found the suspect?"

"Nope. Just thought you'd appreciate being kept in the loop – there's a helicopter on the roof."

Wright froze. The bed sheets he had been ripping off the mattress drifted down to the carpet. "What? Why?"

"It's a news chopper. They're watching HBS in case—"

Damn it! That changed everything. "Get up to the roof!" he yelled. "Caswell, are you hearing this?"

"Yes, sir. You want me up there too?"

"Yes," he said. He was already running towards the stairwell. "You take the lift, Elton takes the stairs. If the suspect knows about the chopper, you can bet that's where she's headed. But Baxter and Mills, keep doing what you're doing. We can't let her slip past. Got it?"

"Copy that."

The stairwell door exploded open as Wright charged through it. He hesitated for a moment to listen, and he did hear footsteps. But they were coming up towards him, not above him and moving away. They would be the other police officers, not the girl. He started running up the stairs.

A helicopter was the one thing that could get out past the roadblock. It would be the girl's best chance at getting out clean. They didn't know her real name, her description could fit a hundred thousand girls in this country, and – Wright swore under his breath as he realized – depending on how long she'd been free when the fire started, she could have wiped her prints off the car.

If she got away now, they had no leads. She could vanish into thin air, and they would have no way to get her back.

The door to the roof was propped open with a rubber wedge. Wright ran through, out into the night. A feeble wind prodded him, rustling in his ears. The sky was stained ocean blue, with ash-grey clouds splattered across the horizon.

The news crew was standing around near the edge of the roof. A girl in headphones stared at Wright, startled. The cameraman turned his head, keeping the bulky camera pointed at the reporter in the spotlight. The reporter himself was the same guy who had interviewed Wright in the alley a few short hours before. A guy who might have been the helicopter pilot was sitting in a fold-out chair.

"Where's the girl?" Wright shouted as he approached.

"Keep rolling!" the girl in headphones said. Then, to Wright: "You're interrupting a shoot. Would you—"

"Where's the girl?" Wright demanded again. "Dark hair, white top, mid-teens. Where is she?"

"There's no one up here," the cameraman interjected. "Just us."

The reporter kept the microphone poised under his chin, patiently waiting for another take. "Is that Detective Wright?" he said. "I interviewed this guy earlier about the body."

Wright scanned the rooftop. A couple of block-like vents, a towering steel aerial. Nowhere for her to hide. "Where's the helicopter?"

"What, our copter?" the girl said. "Over there."

"Do the police have a statement about the apparent car crash at this time, detective?" the reporter asked.

Wright ignored the question, staring at the chopper. It was dark and silent, crouched on the roof like a sleeping dog. "Has anyone come up here?" he asked. "Since you got here?"

"Just you," said headphones. "And those guys."

Wright didn't need to turn to know that Caswell and Elton had emerged from the stairwell behind him.

"Any sign of her, sir?" Elton asked.

Wright stared out across the dark rooftop. "No," he said. "It looks like I was...do you hear that?"

There was a noise. A faint whine, rising in pitch and volume.

"What the hell?" The girl pulled off her headphones. The cameraman looked puzzled.

"No!" Wright sprinted towards the helicopter. The blades were starting to turn.

"Now raise the collective," Benjamin said. "That's the lever to your left. Far left."

The cockpit of the helicopter was covered with lights. Every flat surface was freckled with glowing buttons and dials and switches. It was like being inside a Christmas tree. And it may as well have been a spaceship; Ash had no idea what she was doing.

She pulled up the lever Benjamin had indicated, gently. Nothing appeared to happen. She could see Detective Wright's face at the window, and hoped no one in the film crew had a spare set of keys.

"Nothing happened," she said. "What's it supposed to do?"

"The collective controls altitude," Benjamin said. "If the helicopter isn't rising, the blades aren't spinning fast enough, or you're not pulling hard enough."

Ash shrugged apologetically at Wright. She tried to put on a look that said, *Sorry. I know you're just doing your job. I'm just doing mine.*

Wright didn't look consoled. He pulled out a revolver, but Ash wasn't worried – police weren't allowed to fire on unarmed suspects, and he seemed to be a fairly by-the-book kind of guy. Ash pulled the collective as hard as she could, and his face disappeared from the window as the helicopter lurched up into the sky.

"Whoa, okay, I'm in the air," she said.

The city fanned out underneath her, row after row of lights

blinking into view. The skyline started to curve and spin away to the left. "I'm turning," she said. "I don't want to turn. What do I do?"

"The pedals at your feet control the tail rotor," Benjamin said. "They're very sensitive. Left one turns left, right one turns right."

Ash put a little pressure on the right-hand pedal, and the helicopter turned back around. It was still rising, and was now about level with the top of HBS.

"Okay," Benjamin said. "Ready to cross the street?"

"Yes," Ash said. "Speak up, I can barely hear you."

"The cyclic is the stick in front of you. It controls the tilt of the rotors up above, so it's what you use to move forwards or backwards."

"Which way is which?"

"Ummm…" Benjamin sounded embarrassed. "The book doesn't say."

Ash boggled at the labyrinth of controls in front of her. "Book? What book? When I asked you if you knew how to fly a helicopter, you said yes!"

"Well, what I meant was *The Worst-Case Scenario Survival Handbook* has a chapter on how to *land* a helicopter."

"You're joking," Ash said. "I'm trusting my life to that book?"

"It's been really useful when I'm watching your back," Benjamin said defensively. "You're always getting into trouble."

"You're always putting me in it!" Ash said. "So you're saying you don't know which way I'll move when I push this lever forwards."

"You're high enough now," Benjamin said. "I can see you on TV. So just push it any way and see what the chopper does."

"'See what the chopper does'," Ash muttered. She pushed the cyclic forward.

The helicopter leaned, like a boxer preparing to charge. The apartment building started to slide away underneath it, and Ash lowered the collective a little, trying to lose some height. The HBS building grew in the windscreen.

"You don't want to come in too fast," Benjamin cautioned. "You'll overshoot the HBS roof. Lose some more altitude, and ease off on the cyclic."

Ash pushed down the collective and pulled back the cyclic. The helicopter hovered over the street. Turning her head, she could see the burning apartment, with flames still dangling out the window on the bed-sheet rope.

"Ready to land?" Benjamin asked.

"I can handle it," Ash replied. She pushed the cyclic and the collective, and the helicopter started to drift down towards the HBS roof.

A halogen light swept across the windscreen, and Ash squinted. Apparently someone down below had noticed her up here. Strangely self-conscious, landing a helicopter for the first time while a couple of hundred people and a live television audience watched, she held the levers steady and watched as the roof approached.

She tilted the pedals again, and the helicopter's trajectory curved. She didn't want to hit the big yellow cube.

The rooftop accelerated up to meet her, and she resisted the urge to tug on the collective. She might overshoot the rooftop if she did that.

Thump! The landing skis crunched down on the concrete, and Ash exhaled finally. "I'm on the ground."

Benjamin applauded politely. "Well done."

"How do I switch the rotors off?"

"Not sure. The book is relying on the engine having already stalled."

Ash rolled her eyes, and just did the opposite of what she had done to start it – she took the keys out of the ignition. The motor shuddered to a halt. Ash slid the door open and climbed out.

The rooftop was deserted, but there was plenty of light from the caged spotlights around the cube. Ash walked towards the stairwell door. Then she stopped, and walked back.

She remembered the hit man firing the gun as she drove the Veyron off this roof. She thought one of his shots had hit the cube. And now, as she approached it, she could see the glittering hole.

She touched the side of the cube. It wasn't concrete after all – it was metal. And as she stared at the bullet hole, she realized that it wasn't painted yellow. The metal itself had a brownish sunflower tinge, like...

...like the cube itself was made of gold.

Ash stepped slowly away from it. The cube suddenly seemed imposing, dangerous. She noticed for the first time that there was a small console attached at the bottom, connected by numerous wires. An alarm system.

"Benjamin," she said softly. "I think I just found Buckland's $200 million."

"What? Really? Where? On the rooftop?"

"The gold cube is real gold," she said.

There was a long silence.

"I'm serious," Ash said. "The gunman fired a shot into it, and it's not hollow."

"No way," Benjamin said. "It's huge! There's no way it could be solid gold. That's impossible."

Ash scraped some filaments from the edge of the bullet hole, took out the scanner capsule, tipped it so the fake anthrax fell out, and sprinkled the gold in. "I'm sending you some for analysis," she said.

"No way," Benjamin said. "No way, no way, no – oh."

"Oh what?" Ash said.

"It's gold," Benjamin said. "But it's not just regular cheap-ring gold. It's pure gold. Twenty-four carat. Did you say the whole cube is *solid*?"

"Looks that way," Ash said. She walked around the cube, measuring it with her gaze. "It's about – 6 metres. It has 6-metre sides. Six by six by six to get the volume. What's it worth?"

There was silence in her headphones.

"What's it worth?"

"Shut up a second," Benjamin said. "I'm working it out."

Ash heard him mutter something about gold density, value per kilogram, kilogram per square metre. She took a few steps back to survey the cube again. She looked at her hands. *Now* they were shaking.

"Uh, Ash?" Benjamin sounded scared. "The cube isn't worth $200 million."

Ash's chest felt tight. "How much is it worth?"

"Ninety-five *billion*, nine hundred and seven million, four hundred and twelve thousand, eight hundred dollars."

Ash staggered backwards. Her legs turned to jelly and she landed on the ground with a smack. She was dimly aware of a vein of drool as it slid down her chin. Her palms were sweaty. Her eyes were frozen open.

She was looking at the most money she'd ever seen in her life.

Unmasked

Wright stared across the street to the HBS roof. The helicopter was perched there – and he'd seen the girl's silhouette as she'd jumped down, walked around for a bit, stared at the cube, then fallen over backwards. What the hell was she doing? She had a helicopter, anonymity and the cover of darkness. She had the perfect opportunity to escape scot-free…

…and instead, she'd flown less than 100 metres before landing again, in plain sight.

"TRA had better let us into HBS," the girl in headphones said. "We need that helicopter back."

"You should have thought of that before you left it unlocked with the keys in it," Wright muttered.

He looked across to HBS. Ash was standing up. Dusting herself off. Jogging towards the stairwell entrance.

"We were within 20 metres of it," the girl retorted, "and helicopters, by the way, are not easy to fly. Plus, we were told the building was deserted and in a quarantined area. Not exactly a hotspot for thieves."

"I'm standing on the roof of Shine Apartments," the reporter was saying to the camera, "across the street from the HBS building, where there's been a dramatic development. A short time ago witnesses stood transfixed as a car flew off the roof of HBS and crash-landed inside one of the apartments opposite. Only moments ago, a helicopter was hijacked from this very rooftop and flown across the street, landing on HBS. It has been speculated that the culprit may have been the driver of the car, having miraculously survived the crash."

"A helicopter was hijacked," Wright thought. Carefully put. Can't have their viewers knowing that it was their helicopter, stolen due to their negligence.

His phone rang. He held it against his ear. "Yeah?"

"Damien," Belle said. "Fill me in."

"The driver of the car was a teenage girl," Wright said. "She wasn't hurt in the crash, but she tried to hide from us – I found her in an apartment bathroom. She told me there's a government assassin inside HBS, hunting Hammond Buckland, and that he's the one who shot at her as she drove off the roof. She refused to explain what she was doing in HBS, why Hammond Buckland's car was on the roof, or how she got his keys. She escaped custody, and made it to the roof. Just my luck, there was a news team up here. They were dumb enough to leave their chopper unlocked. The girl stole it and – this is the weird part – she flew it back across the street to HBS and has just re-entered the building."

"*That's* the weird part? Right. What's with the fire on the sixteenth floor?"

"Oh, yeah," Wright said. "That was part of her escape plan. She used it as a distraction."

"Teenagers," Belle said. "What do you think of her story?"

"The government assassinating Buckland?" Wright shrugged. "It's unlikely. Ridiculous, even. But this has been an unlikely and ridiculous day, so it almost seems to fit."

"You got any better theories?"

Wright rubbed his eyes. "No. I need more people to interview. So far all I've had is a brief off-the-record chat with a girl who knows way more than she was willing to tell. I need to get inside HBS. I need to arrest everybody, and talk to them one by one until I can see the whole picture. But TRA won't let me, because they're in it up to their necks too."

"Now get some filler footage of the helicopter," the girl in headphones was shouting at the cameraman. "Do it from the north corner, so you can't see our logo on the side."

The reporter was talking on his phone. "Yeah, a few technical hitches. But the story's getting bigger. Send another team, get them to hover around HBS and wait."

"You think the terrorist threat is real?" Belle asked.

"Nope," Wright said. "That'd just be another coincidence to throw onto the pile. It seems far more likely that the government made it up to cover whatever it is they're trying to pull here."

"Then go inside," she said. "If there's no exposure risk, go inside HBS and prove it, before the players have a chance to finish their games and disappear."

"They're armed, Belle. They've threatened to open fire on anyone who approaches the entrance. And they'll do it, too – it'd be suspicious if they didn't, and I've got a dead body to prove that whatever they're fighting over is worth killing for."

"The girl got inside, didn't she?"

"She had a helicopter," Wright said. "I don't."

"You're a policeman. She's not."

"I can't call in a police chopper to violate quarantine."

"Sure you can," Belle said. "You just have to say the magic words."

"What are—" Wright broke off. She was right. There was a way to do it.

"I'll call you back," he said.

TRA's power stemmed from anti-terrorism legislation, which declared that when terrorists were suspected to have infiltrated any organization, that organization would be stripped of its authority until the breach was found. TRA was able to take over any organization at all, including businesses, law-enforcement agencies, schools and charities.

But there was a way to use this power against them.

Wright dialled a number in his phone and hit SEND.

A voice answered. Bored-sounding. One of the good, perfectly capable officers forced to stay at the station because of the raised terror-alert level. Wright smiled. He was about to make the officer's day.

"I need a helicopter and an attack team to the rooftop of Shine Apartments right away," he said.

"Sir, that building is inside the quarantine zone. We don't have jurisdiction, and therefore can't enter without TRA sanction."

Wright then said the magic words. "TRA has been compromised."

* * *

One more piece of the puzzle had snapped into place. All day, Ash had found it hard to believe that the government would go to so much effort and risk so much for only $2.2 billion. That might seem like a spectacular amount of money to her and Benjamin, but to most governments it was a mere droplet in their bathtub-sized coffers.

But Hammond Buckland had somehow accumulated almost $96 billion, and then hidden it in plain sight. That was enough to get anyone and everyone who knew about it searching. And suddenly Ash felt way out of her depth. It was like being a cheetah chasing a fat gazelle, and then stumbling into a clearing where Tyrannosaurus rexes were attacking a giant Brachiosaurus.

She barely remembered pushing through the stairwell door, running down the first flight of steps, pushing against the wall and sliding to her knees. It was like someone had hit MUTE on her life. Nothing seemed quite real.

"You know what?" Benjamin said in her ear. "That cube is going to be really hard to steal."

Ash snorted. "You think?"

"I ran the calculations again to get the weight – it should be around 4169 tonnes."

"Sure won't fit in my handbag," Ash muttered. "I would've preferred diamonds, or bearer bonds."

"But there's a bright side," Benjamin said. "Gold is easier

to trade for cash than either of those things. It retains its value well. And because it's a soft metal, you could scrape some out of the cube and put it in the helicopter quite easily. It's worth about $23,000 per kilogram, and the chopper can carry about a tonne. So you could get away with $23 million."

"And leave ninety-five billion, eight hundred and eighty-four million, four hundred and twelve thousand, eight hundred dollars sitting up there on the roof?" Ash demanded. "Just forget we ever found it?"

"Do you really need it?" Benjamin asked. "What the hell would you spend it on?"

"I—"

"That's why it's up there," Benjamin continued. "Because Buckland doesn't need it, doesn't want it, and can't get rid of it. It's brought him nothing but trouble, and even if we could take it, it would do the same thing to us!"

Ash thumped her fist against the stairwell wall. "Yeah, but could you live with yourself? Knowing you could've had more money than Bill Gates and J.K. Rowling put together, but you turned it down?"

"With $23 million as the consolation prize?" Benjamin said. "Yeah, I think I could!"

Ash put her head in her hands.

"Don't get greedy," Benjamin warned. "Remember how thieves get busted."

They try to take more than they can carry, Ash thought.

"All right," she said. "I'll find something to carve up the gold with, and then I'll go back and take as much as will fit in the helicopter. Deal?"

"Deal," Benjamin said.

"Wait. Will they try to shoot me down if I leave in the helicopter? Violating quarantine?"

"I don't think so. They know the anthrax is fake, and it's a fair bet they've sealed Buckland in somewhere, so they know it won't be him in the chopper. From their point of view, the risks of shooting you down outweigh the risks of letting you go."

Sealed Buckland in. A finger of guilt prodded Ash's heart. She wondered if there was something she could possibly do to save him.

"Don't think about it, Ash," Benjamin warned, sensing her thoughts. "If it helps, the reason Buckland has $93 billion more than we thought he did is probably because not all his ventures are legal. For one thing, he should have paid half of it in tax. For another, do you remember that 'string of high-profile robberies of other banks' that Keighley was talking about? I'm now fairly certain that Buckland was behind them. He arranged them to make all the other banks look bad so more customers would choose HBS National, and then kept the loot for himself. Fraud, theft and tax evasion. You don't owe him anything, Ash. Hammond Buckland is a criminal."

"So are we," she said.

It was a moot point, of course. She didn't know where Buckland was, or where the people trying to kill him were. There was nothing she could do. Ash sighed. There'd be plenty of time to wrestle with her conscience when she was rich.

She was on the landing of the 25th floor. She figured that floor was as good as any to find something to carve up the gold with. There'd be a break room with a knife in it somewhere. Gold was so soft almost any knife would do. Ash wondered how she would defuse the alarm system.

She pulled open the stairwell door.

There was a woman in a hazard suit on the other side of it, mask off, hood down, holding a Heckler & Koch MP5. She pointed the thick barrel at Ash.

"Don't move," she said.

Ash dived backwards and tried to pull the door closed. The woman blocked it with her foot and slammed the butt of the gun into Ash's temple. Ash started to fall backwards down the stairs, but the woman grabbed her by the hair and dragged her back to her feet.

"Perhaps you didn't hear me," the woman said. "Don't move."

Ash tried to breathe evenly. Her scalp felt like it was being torn from her skull. "Okay," she said. "Okay."

The woman smiled. Plastic lips stretched back over hospital-white teeth. She released Ash's hair and gripped her arm instead. "My name is Alex de Totth," she said. "And I'm going to ask you a few questions."

Ash stumbled forward as de Totth started walking. She fell to the floor, but de Totth didn't slow down, so she was dragged for a bit before she could scramble back up.

"I'd heard they were recruiting teenagers," de Totth said. "The theory is that people like me will show mercy to children. The theory is wrong."

Ash grabbed at de Totth's wrist, trying to pull herself up and dull the pain. De Totth slapped Ash's hands away with the butt of the MP5.

"What you have to remember," de Totth said, "is that when you were trained for these situations, your teachers had an agenda."

Trained? Teachers? "What are you—"

De Totth silenced her with a particularly violent tug. "They wanted to keep their secrets. They wanted you not to talk."

Oh, no. No, no, no.

"Oh god," Benjamin said. "Ash, run!"

The headphones fell from her ears as she stumbled again.

"So I'm going to give you what your teachers never did," de Totth continued. "An unbiased assessment of your situation."

She dropped the MP5 as she reached Keighley's desk. It swung out on a black bungee cord as she reached down and grasped Ash by the throat with one hand and the leg with the other. De Totth lifted her up, dumped her on top of the desk, and caught the gun as it bounced back up.

"You cooperate, you live," de Totth said. "You don't, you die." She smiled again. "Simple, right? Here are the specifics."

Ash tried to roll off the desk, but de Totth smacked her face with a gloved palm and held her down.

"The other government agent," de Totth said. "I don't know why I was ordered to let him out of the oil vat. I don't know why I'm only permitted to use tranq ammo on him. I also don't know where he is, and that's the information I'm looking for. So I'm going to ask you."

What the heck is she on about? Ash thought wildly. Oil vat? Tranq ammo? The other agent?

"There are three possible answers you can give me," de Totth said. "One: you give me his exact location. I'll let you go. I have nothing to lose from that. Two: you refuse to tell me. I'll put the barrel of my gun against the little toe on your right foot and shoot it off. Then I'll ask again, and if I get the same response, I'll choose another toe. Once I run out of toes, I'll start on fingers. Once you have no more fingers, I'll take one of your ears – but only one, because I'm going to keep asking the question and keep shooting body parts, and I need you to be able to hear me. Got it?"

Ash felt sick. Like she'd swallowed cement mix and it was hardening inside her. She wanted to look around for ways out of this, but she couldn't take her eyes off the gun.

"Three: you tell me you don't know where he is, you don't know what I'm talking about – anything like that. If I think you're lying to me, I'll take a toe, finger or ear. But if you say it convincingly enough, and I believe you…"

"I don't—" Ash began shakily.

"…then I'll kill you," de Totth continued, "because that means you're absolutely useless to me." She ripped off Ash's shoe and clicked off the safety catch on her gun. "Ready to start?"

Peachey reached the 25th floor, and eased the stairwell door open. The first thing he saw was a SIG Sauer 9 mm pistol with the safety catch off.

The second thing he saw was Adam Keighley holding it.

Peachey's eyes widened. What the hell was this?

His first thought was that Keighley worked security for

Buckland as well as being a secretary. But that made no sense. Buckland already had security, and besides, security shouted "Halt!" or "Freeze!". They didn't just take aim silently, grim concentration on their faces.

His next guess was that Keighley was an undercover cop. They were tougher than security guards and, as a general rule, a little more relaxed about the rules and etiquette of shooting someone. They could get away with a lot by explaining that they were "only maintaining their cover".

This day had been so insane that it seemed anything was possible. Peachey wouldn't have been surprised if Keighley turned out to be an alien protecting the mother ship concealed in the basement. But it was his third thought that made the most sense to him.

It had baffled him all day how Buckland had seemed to know he was coming, when Walker had said that the operation had only been planned a few days ago. On the one hand, Buckland couldn't possibly have improvised his many traps so quickly, but on the other, why would Walker lie about something like that?

Now Peachey thought he had found a third possibility. He didn't understand the *why* of it just yet, but he thought he'd grasped the *how*.

Buckland had seen it coming because he had forced it to happen.

Whatever reason the government had for wanting him killed, he knew about it. So he forced their hand, making sure he knew when the hitter would be coming. The best form of defence is attack. Maybe he had decided to retire or planned a trip overseas or something. Either way, he told no one except his closest, most trusted employees. Knowing that at least one of them was a government agent.

If Adam Keighley was one of Walker's men, that would explain how Walker had managed to hack into the CCTV footage. And it would explain how Walker had been able to track Peachey's movements; he remembered Keighley spraying his – Ford's – name tag with something to "activate" it. Microdots, most likely, so the government could keep tabs on him. And it would explain how Buckland had managed to stay a step ahead the whole way – he'd been controlling the information that got to Keighley, so Keighley passed on only certain things to Walker, and Walker passed them on to Peachey.

Keighley being a government agent made perfect sense. After all, he wasn't pointing the SIG at Peachey. He hadn't even noticed the lift doors opening, as far as Peachey could tell. He was pointing it down the corridor, at someone Peachey couldn't see from where he was.

* * *

"Where is the other government agent?" de Totth asked.

She thinks I'm working for the government, Ash thought. Her mind was racing. That means she doesn't work for the government herself. She works for Buckland! The TRA aren't the real TRA, they're here to protect Buckland!

"Sorry," de Totth said. "I should have clarified this. Silence counts as refusing to tell me." She wrapped her gloved fingers around Ash's toe, holding it in place.

"I don't work for the government!" Ash said. "I'm on your side!"

"Wrong answer," de Totth said, pressing the barrel of the gun against Ash's toe.

"No! Wait!" Ash said.

The barrel was cold against her skin. De Totth ignored her.

"Wait!" she said again. "I'll help you!"

De Totth paused. Okay, Ash thought. How do I get out of this?

"You were right," Ash said. "I'm a government agent. I don't know where he is, but—"

De Totth's finger tightened on the trigger.

"*But*," Ash said, desperate, "I can contact him."

"Tell me how," de Totth said.

"My iPod headphones. They're connected to a phone in my back pocket. He's on the other end of the line."

"You can make him come to get you?"

Ash took a deep breath. "No, but maybe you can. He outranks me, he's not supposed to follow my instructions. But if you told him you had captured me and made him believe that I was giving you information, he might show up. To silence me."

De Totth examined Ash with inky black eyes. She stood there for what felt like a long time. Ash's breathing came in ragged gasps.

"Okay," de Totth said. "Give me the phone."

Ash rolled onto her side so she could reach her back pocket. She withdrew the phone slowly. I sure hope Benjamin heard all that, she thought. And that he'll be able to play along.

Ash held out the phone, but de Totth didn't take it. She was staring into space, like she was listening carefully, or trying to tell the direction of the wind.

"Trap," she growled.

She started to turn, lifting the MP5 from Ash's toe and clicking the safety from semi to auto. But she didn't make it.

Ash screamed as pink mist puffed out from the back of de Totth's head. Hot wetness spattered Ash's face, and she gagged. The bullet kept going, thunking into the wall behind her. Only then did she hear the gunshots from the corridor behind de Totth – she rolled off Keighley's desk and landed on all fours behind it.

Crack! Crack! Slugs slammed against the side of the desk but didn't penetrate. She heard a thud as de Totth's body hit the ground. The shots kept coming, either because the shooter wanted to be certain that Alex de Totth was really dead, or because he was hoping to hit Ash through the desk.

Peachey watched as Keighley fired shot after shot down the corridor in quick succession. The guy's undercover work was obviously much better than his marksmanship.

The gun clicked empty.

"Hello," Peachey said.

Keighley whirled around, pointing the gun. "You!" he said.

"Me," Peachey said. "Did you hit anything, or is it early days? I'd lend you some bullets, but I think I might be fresh out."

"I'm doing your job, Peachey," Keighley hissed. "How about you take over?"

"You mean after all those shots, Buckland is still alive?"

Keighley pointed. "That was Alex de Totth, Buckland's main bodyguard. So now that I've done the hard part for you, how about you finally do what we're paying you to do?"

Keighley killed de Totth? No way. Peachey stepped out of the lift and stared down the corridor. There she was, in front of a colander-like reception desk, with at least three gunshot wounds, including one just above her left eye. She was dead, all right.

"Buckland's in his office," Keighley said. "Unarmed, and unguarded. Don't screw up this time." He stepped into the lift, pushed a button and the doors swept shut.

Peachey scanned the floor for de Totth's gun, but it seemed to have disappeared. No matter. He suspected Keighley was probably right – he had done the hard part. Without de Totth, the rest of her team would evacuate. If Buckland was in his office, Peachey would be able to kill him with his bare hands.

The part about de Totth working for Buckland didn't seem to quite fit. Why had she let him out of the deep fryer if that was the case? But Peachey figured it was time he stopped worrying about everyone else's motives and finally finished the day's work.

Wright waved his arms in the air, signalling to the police helicopter. The rooftop was swept clean of litter and dust as it swung in to land.

"Do you mind?" the girl in headphones roared. "We're recording cut footage over here!"

"Relax," said the reporter. "These shots won't have audio."

"Do you want us to come with you across to HBS, sir?" Caswell asked Wright.

"The assault team will be all the manpower I need," Wright said, "and once the building's empty we can all have a look around. I need you and the others here tracing the girl's path, trying to find a clear print."

"Don't we already have that from the car, sir?"

Wright sighed. "I'm betting she wiped down the car."

Caswell raised an eyebrow but said nothing. He hadn't met the girl, so he didn't understand. Wright had her figured as a genius or a lunatic. Maybe both. But definitely smart enough to clean the car on her way out.

The thundering of helicopter blades discouraged further discussion. The landing skis clanked against the roof, but the blades didn't slow down – the attack team wasn't getting out. This was only a temporary stop to pick up Wright.

Wright raised a hand by way of farewell and jogged over to the chopper. The hold door ground open as he approached it.

"Detective Wright?" a masked and goggled man yelled, cradling a Remington 870 shotgun.

"Yeah," Wright shouted as he clambered in.

"We were hoping you could brief us on the situation on the way over," the man said.

"You'd have to go around the block a few times," Wright replied.

* * *

Ash had heard the conversation between Keighley and "Peachey" from a safe distance away. When she'd heard the click of an empty gun, she had slipped out from behind the desk. De Totth's MP5 had landed a couple of metres away from her body – Ash grabbed it. She had no idea how to use it, but she didn't want the assassin to have it. She ran around the corner. Apparently neither man had spotted her.

She was still shivering. She hadn't been injured in her encounter with de Totth, but it had been a close call. The image of her toes being shot off one by one would haunt her nightmares for years. And every time she shut her eyes, she saw de Totth's head twitch as the bullet punched through it. She folded her arms over her chest to banish the cold. It was futile; the shivers were coming from within.

Okay, she thought. Keighley is a government agent. He gets the job as Buckland's secretary, and finds out that Buckland is planning to leave the country. He reports this to his superiors, and they hire a hit man to kill Buckland – that's this guy named Peachey. But Peachey "screws up" somehow, and gives Buckland time to call in his backup. Buckland has planted some fake anthrax under his office, and calls his team of mercenaries disguised as TRA, led by Alex de Totth. That keeps the cops out of HBS and his employees out of the crossfire as the mercenaries and Peachey fight it out.

Why actually plant fake anthrax? Ash wondered. Why not just make the call? Was he hoping someone else would find it?

Doesn't matter – I messed it up, Ash thought. De Totth mistook me for a government agent, since I wasn't one of hers and I wasn't a cop and I wasn't an employee. She tried to use me to find out where "the other government agent" was. At the time I thought she meant the hit man, Peachey – but now I'm pretty sure she meant Keighley, who is presumably instructed to finish the job if Peachey fails.

So while de Totth was distracted with me, Keighley managed to get behind her. Now she's dead, and Buckland is defenceless.

Because of me.

Ash put the headphones back in her ears, and heard only silence. "Benjamin?" she whispered.

"Ash! Thank goodness. I thought…are you hit?"

"No," Ash said, "just freaked out. Did you hear that conversation between Keighley and the hitter?"

"Bits of it. So de Totth and her fake TRA team work for Buckland, not the government, right?"

"Right," Ash said. "And I'm pretty sure Buckland planted the fake anthrax to get them in here. But now de Totth's dead and her team is missing."

"So, Buckland…"

"Is screwed, yeah," Ash confirmed.

There was a pause.

"It's not your fault, Ash," Benjamin said gently.

"If I hadn't come here, de Totth would still be alive and Buckland might have a chance," Ash hissed. "That sounds like it's my fault to me."

"Don't be stupid. You may as well blame Peachey's mother for giving birth to him. You're not the one about to kill Buckland, and you didn't intentionally create the circumstances leading to his death. It is *not your fault*."

Ash heard Peachey's footsteps as he walked up the corridor to Buckland's office. She flattened herself against the wall as he walked past. "Maybe not," she whispered. "But maybe I can stop it." She slipped out from behind the corner and followed Peachey towards Buckland's office.

Defiance

"Why is he just standing there?" the assault team leader shouted.

The helicopter was drawing a giant spiral in the sky, slowly looping in towards the HBS rooftop. The night was moonless, so the many city lights below provided the only illumination. The yellow cube glowed in the halogen lights on the roof.

The lights were on in several HBS offices, and Wright could see the employees lounging against sofas and desks. Their panic had dissipated, leaving only resignation and boredom. Ties were loosened, sleeves rolled up, watches frequently checked.

But Wright wasn't looking at them. He was staring through the empty window frame, into Hammond Buckland's office. The water lapped gently at the edges of the spa. The papers on the desk fluttered in the breeze. And Buckland stood with his back to the window, perfectly still.

If Buckland had confined himself there once the quarantine had started, Wright would have expected him to be either pacing nervously or sitting down. Perhaps even working at the computer. And if the girl was right, and there were people in the building trying to kill him, he should be hiding under the desk. Or, again, pacing nervously.

But he was just standing there, the wind ruffling his hair, hands in his pockets. Like he'd been sentenced to death, but he'd had time to get used to it. Wright wished he could see his face.

"What's he doing?" the leader shouted.

"I have no idea," Wright replied.

Adam Keighley opened the lift doors again. He wanted to follow Peachey to the office unseen. It was his job to send confirmation of the hit to Walker.

As he stepped out into the corridor, he saw that someone was already following Peachey. Ashley Arthur. What the hell was she still doing here?

Keighley wondered briefly if he should stop her. There had been enough mistakes already today, and he didn't want her messing things up. He was out of bullets, but he could always strangle her, smother her, break her neck.

Trouble was, Peachey would almost certainly hear him do it. And Keighley didn't want Peachey to know he was being followed. Better for him to believe that Walker was relying on his word to establish Buckland's death. Better for him to think that if he failed, there was no contingency plan.

And besides, Peachey creeped Keighley out. He was unpredictable and violent. Better that he didn't know Keighley was behind him.

Keighley watched as Peachey opened the door to Buckland's office and stepped through. Ashley crept slowly past the reception desk.

Leave her alone, Keighley decided. How much of a threat could a teenage girl be?

He leaned against the wall and waited to hear the gunshots.

Peachey closed the door behind him.

"You're late," Buckland said.

Peachey was about to charge towards him, but he noticed two things. One: Buckland appeared to be unarmed. Two: the

Glock he'd discarded when breaking the window that morning was lying exactly where he'd left it, under one of the chairs. He scooped it up, ejected the magazine, checked that there were still bullets in it. There were. He snapped it back in, clicked the safety off, and pointed it back at Buckland. The whole process took less than two seconds.

"I agree," he said.

"But still," Buckland continued, "I am impressed. You passed."

Peachey raised an eyebrow. He'd had some weird people say some weird things to try to talk him out of killing them. But this was the beginning of something he'd never heard before – and he'd never seen a victim this calm.

"There's nothing you can say to stop me from killing you," he said.

"I have a job for you," Buckland replied.

Ash took a deep breath outside the door. She checked her hands. They were shaking so much they were almost blurry.

She didn't know what was going on inside. She knew Peachey was in there, probably Buckland, and potentially anyone else from mercenaries to police. She didn't know what Peachey was armed with. It could be sharp or blunt – either was dangerous in those hands. Worse, it could be a firearm, and Ash thought she'd probably used up her nine lives where dodging bullets was concerned.

But she knew that only hours ago she'd bludgeoned Peachey unconscious with nothing but a pair of bolt cutters and the element of surprise. And she still had both those things.

She gripped the handle and turned it slowly. She was awash with the sudden fear that someone on the other side was watching it turn, waiting for her to open it, just a crack, so they could take aim and blow her head off.

She heard the soft click of the lock. She pushed the door open gradually.

"Goddamn it," the team leader said. "We have a situation."

Wright watched from inside the helicopter, knuckles white around the binoculars. There was a man in Buckland's office, pointing a gun at Buckland. He hadn't been carrying the gun when he entered – he'd found it on the floor. Buckland hadn't reacted at all, as far as Wright could see. What was going on?

A member of the assault team was quickly assembling a sniper rifle out of a box. "I'm on it, sir," she said. "Give me thirty seconds, I'll be ready to take a shot."

"Good," the leader said. "But hold your fire until I give the order."

"Understood."

Wright saw the door handle turn, and the door open a crack. He squinted.

The girl's face edged into view.

"Oh, no," he said. "No." Then, to the leader: "We have another civilian in the room, repeat, civilian in the room."

"Keep it steady," the sniper roared at the pilot.

Peachey could hear a helicopter outside, blades pounding over the wind. But he couldn't see it in the darkness. Maybe it was de Totth's team pulling out.

"I already have a job," he growled.

"Mine pays better," Buckland said. "I'll give you ten billion now, another ten when the job is done."

He was moving, walking slowly and calmly from the desk, past the spa, towards the painting on the wall.

"Stop right there," Peachey said.

"Originally, I didn't think you would be up to it," Buckland said. "Then I tried to kill you, and discovered how hard it was. The gas, the water tank, the deep fryer – I have to say, you're one tough—"

"I said stop," Peachey said, and Buckland obeyed. He raised his hands and smiled.

"Are you going to shoot me? Throw away $20 billion?"

"I always complete my mission," Peachey said.

"You have a new mission now," Buckland replied. "Put down the gun, and I'll brief you."

Was he serious? Peachey stared at Buckland's golden eyes. They held his gaze too frigidly, too compulsively.

A smile spread across Peachey's face. "You're bluffing," he said.

Ash crept towards Peachey's back. She remembered that he'd taken two blows before losing consciousness last time, and vowed to give him at least three to make sure.

She raised the bolt cutters. She was four steps away from him.

One.

"There's no job," Peachey said.

Two.

"You'll tell whatever lie you think will save you."

Three.

"But no matter what you do, no matter what you say, you have only seconds left to live."

Four...

Ash gripped the handle tightly, and started to—

Buckland was shaking his head. He was looking at Peachey but Ash suddenly sensed that the gesture was intended for her.

"No," he said. "Don't do it."

The girl was too close to the guy with the gun. The sniper wasn't ready yet. But when she was, if the girl was still standing there, the sniper wouldn't be able to take a shot without the risk of hitting her.

"Come on, Ash," Wright whispered. "Get out of the way."

"Nearly ready?" the leader asked.

"Fifteen seconds," the sniper said without looking up. She snapped the barrel into place.

"You are about to make a very stupid decision," Buckland warned.

Peachey smiled. This was what he wanted. He wanted to hear the fear in the billionaire's voice.

"You've already made too many," he replied.

"Your employer isn't really a government agent – he works for me," Buckland said. He was starting to sound desperate. "I hired him to test you. Kill me, and you don't get paid."

"The agent was a woman," Peachey said smugly. "Nice try. Is there anyone you'd like me to pass your goodbyes on to?"

* * *

Keighley pressed his ear against the door. He hadn't heard any shots yet, and he thought he detected the mumbling of voices. Do your job, Peachey, he thought. Do it.

Ash backed away. What's wrong? she thought. I'm his only chance – the hit man's not buying his story. Why doesn't he want saving?

"If you're planning on pulling that trigger, you'd best say your own goodbyes," Buckland said. "Because you're going straight to prison. This area has been quarantined, remember? There are police roadblocks all around. There's no way out."

"Time's a factor," Wright said. The girl was moving back from the guy with the gun.

"Almost ready," the sniper said. She lay down on the floor of the chopper and nestled the stock in the crook of her arm.

"Mission complete," Peachey said.

"No," Buckland said. "No, don't—"

Crack.

Wright saw the muzzle flash from the guy's gun, and the firework of blood as the first shot burst through Buckland's left shoulder blade.

"Goddamn it! Open fire, now!"

Crack.

Torso right. Peachey barely saw the second shot puncture the right breast of Buckland's suit – he was already taking aim at the head.

Crack.

Ash watched with horror as Buckland's head twisted backwards, like someone had grabbed him by the hair and tugged. His legs gave way instantly, and he toppled backwards, crumbling down, into the spa.

Dust

Ash couldn't take her eyes off the spa. Buckland was only visible in the water for a moment before the water turned dark, clouds of blood billowing through it. Buckland had tripped over the switches for the jets as he fell in, and now the water bubbled sickeningly.

The hit man was keeping his gun trained on the water, checking that Buckland wasn't coming back up.

He wasn't. Two shots to the chest and one to the head – Buckland would have been dead before he hit the water.

Ash started to back away, slowly. Maybe she could make

it out the door before Peachey turned around. One step, two steps...

Peachey's body turned before his gaze, which hovered over the water for a second longer. Ash put her hand on the door handle.

He saw her.

His eyes widened with recognition and astonishment. Ash remembered that the last time he'd seen her she'd been flying off the top of HBS in a Bugatti Veyron. He must have assumed she was dead.

He raised the gun, and Ash found herself staring down the barrel. She didn't have time to get out of the way before he pulled the trigger.

Click.

No more bullets.

Ash stood frozen for a moment. She willed her legs to take her out the door, but it was like they were manacled to the floor.

Peachey laughed. He wiped his prints off the gun and tossed it into the water.

"You," he told Ash, "might just be the luckiest girl alive."

Then he walked past her, pulled the door open, and left. The door swung slowly shut behind him.

Ash fell to her knees. It wasn't intended as a dramatic gesture – her legs just gave way. She put her hands on the carpet, which was freckled with droplets from the pool.

What do I do now? she asked herself. What do I do?

Keighley watched Peachey leave the office. He hit SEND on his phone and pressed it to his ear.

"I'm listening," Tania Walker said.

"The job is done," Keighley said. He hung up – no more needed to be said.

"We need to get over there," Wright said. "Are you in touch with the officers on the perimeter?"

"Sure," the leader said.

"Make sure they don't let anyone through," Wright said. "No one. Everyone involved in this fiasco is right here, and I want to keep it that way."

"Got it."

It was at that moment that the yellow cube on the roof of HBS exploded.

Wright fell backwards into the cabin of the helicopter as the flash lit up the sky, and the force of the blast rippled outwards. When he looked up again, he saw that the cube had turned to dust, and was raining down from the heavens like a giant shower of sparks. The spotlights on the top of HBS shimmered through the cascading particles, which shone like gold as the light caught them.

Wright frowned. Actually, it really did look like gold.

The people in the quarantine zone below stared up in confusion as the noise of the explosion dissipated into nothing and the first of the dust particles hit the ground. The streets were full of people crouching to examine the debris, then looking up again and stretching their arms towards the sky, trying to catch some of the gold rain.

A few particles, sucked up by the helicopter blades, wafted in through the cargo door. Wright pressed his fingertip against one to pick it up, and stared at it.

As far as he could tell, yes, it was real gold.

Some of the gold dust was blown over the edge of the quarantine zone by the breeze, reaching the crowds on the other side of the roadblock. There was the same initial pause as the people examined the dust, and then the upwards stare of astonishment. And then they pushed forward, fighting the police with more energy than before, trying to break into the quarantine zone, money rain motivating them more than fear for friends and loved ones had.

Police officers were shoved aside, concrete road barriers were toppled, and thousands of people ran towards HBS, scooping the dust up from the concrete, catching it in their hands and on their faces, stuffing it into their pockets.

Belle's going to freak when she hears about this, Wright thought.

Ash had heard the crack of the explosion, and could see the yellowish dust pouring down past the window, but hadn't worked out what had happened until now.

"No," she said. "No. No. No, no, *no*!"

Buckland had found a way to dispose of his $96 billion. He was sharing it with the people.

Ash had the sudden paranoia that Buckland wasn't dead; that he was somewhere out there laughing at her. She knew it couldn't be true, she'd seen him die, but...

Had she?

Ash crawled towards the spa, switched off the jets, and dipped her arms in. She flattened her hands against the bottom, searching for Buckland's body. The water was shallow, shallower than she remembered.

She ran her fingers all over the bottom of the pool. She found a Glock 7 pistol, but nothing else. There was no sign of Buckland's body.

Ash whirled around, splashing bloody water across the carpet. The room was still empty. Buckland had vanished into thin air.

Could he have climbed out while she was staring out the

window, and snuck out the door behind her? No way. She would have heard him.

The room wasn't as she'd last seen it, she suddenly realized. The scuba suit she'd noticed this morning had gone.

The water was shallower than she'd remembered. The scuba suit was gone. So was Buckland. But where?

Ash felt like she was on the brink of a realization, but couldn't quite wrap her head around it. Until she peered out the window, looking down into the street again, and saw the rest of the fake TRA team. They were still in their hazard suits, goggles on, hoods up, carrying the box of fake anthrax towards their truck. They'd wrapped it in a giant plastic bag and were carrying it with great care, ignoring the people scrabbling for the gold dust. They put the box in the back of their truck, and climbed inside.

Ash watched the truck as it started to move, driving towards the roadblock.

Water shallower.

Scuba suit gone.

Coffin-sized box, taken away.

The driver flashed some ID at one of the struggling cops on the roadblock, who waved the truck through with little hesitation.

Hammond Buckland had faked his own death, Ash

realized. He had staged his murder so well that even the supposed murderer thought he was dead. That's why he didn't want her whacking Peachey over the head. Peachey had to think he was dead too for the trick to work.

She jumped into the pool and started stamping down on the tiles, one at a time. This was the only way Buckland could have escaped. There must be a—

Ash jumped back as a hole opened up in the floor of the pool. Water whirlpooled around her legs, draining into it, pouring down into the room below, where it splattered against the mound of fake anthrax, turning it into soggy grey slush.

Ash jumped back out of the spa and watched it drain itself completely dry. She guessed there must be some kind of switch to close the hole from the other side.

She sat down on the floor, and laughed.

Peachey sipped his macadamia nut latte at the table by the window, watching the chaos from a distance. People were still scraping gold out of cracks in the pavement, cars were still trapped at the intersection, and the police were still trying to get the crowd to disperse.

He'd made it out of HBS without any trouble – since the fake TRA agents were no longer guarding the entrances, the more enterprising members of the public were storming in through the doors, hoping to reach the roof where there was presumably lots more gold dust. Some of the HBS employees, confused and frightened, had given up waiting in their offices and were moving in the other direction, trying to escape. Peachey had slipped through the crowd unnoticed.

When he was outside, he'd edged towards the fallen roadblocks while the police officer nearest him was looking the other way. Then, when the guy looked at him, Peachey started moving back towards HBS, like he was trying to get into the quarantine zone rather than out. Sure enough, the cop grabbed him and threw him over the safety line, telling him to go away, there was nothing to see here. Peachey was free to wander down the street in search of a good coffee shop, like he did after all his jobs.

This particular shop was doing great business. Many of the people who'd tried to get into the quarantine zone and been turned away seemed to be looking for a caffeine hit – Peachey was one of very few customers sitting with a free seat opposite him.

And not any more, he realized, annoyed. Someone was sitting down. He turned to the window, hoping the guy wouldn't try talking to him.

"Good evening, Peachey."

Peachey turned his head back. At first he didn't recognize the man sitting opposite him. He'd shaved his head, and he was wearing different clothes. He was pale, as if he was wearing make-up – or perhaps like he'd been wearing it all the time and had only now scrubbed it off. It was Hammond Buckland.

Peachey was not a superstitious man. But it only takes one ghost to convince you that they're real.

"You're dead," he whispered.

Buckland smiled. "So everyone believes. Thanks to you. They'll go on believing it until they can't find my body, and I'll be long gone by then."

"I killed you," Peachey said. "I shot you."

"With blanks. Did you even wonder why I left your gun right there on the floor of my office? Didn't you think it was strange that Alex de Totth was firing tranquillizer darts at you, and that she left you alone after taking away your Beretta?" He chuckled. "Actually, I only hired her so *you* would kill her. Otherwise the government would send her after me when they realized you had failed. I had no idea Adam Keighley, of all people, would do the job for me. I feel a little short-changed, actually. Do you know how much it costs to hire the world's number-one hit woman for a whole six months?"

"I saw the bullet holes in you!" Peachey's voice was shaky, weak. Confusion replacing shock.

"That's a disadvantage of firing the same three shots into

every victim," Buckland said. "It's easy to pretend to be hit."

Peachey gritted his teeth. If the job wasn't done yet, so be it. He would finish it now. He lunged forward and wrapped his hands around Buckland's throat to squeeze that smug smile out of him—

Only he didn't. He couldn't move from his chair. He couldn't even lift his arms.

"Oh yes," Buckland said. "The drug I had the staff slip into your drink should have kicked in by now. Don't worry, the paralysis should wear off in an hour or two. I own every coffee shop on this street, you see – and I had plenty of pictures of you from the surveillance footage to give them, so they knew who to give the special order to." He shook his head. "And that's a disadvantage of staying nearby for a coffee after a mission. You see where routine gets you?"

"I...will...*kill...you*," Peachey growled. His lips were stiff, and the words came out slurred.

"You just don't get it, do you?" Buckland said. "You won't. You can't. And that's the reason I'm here."

He leaned forward. "I need everyone to know – government, business rivals, gangs, criminals, everyone – that anyone they send after me will be crushed and defeated as totally as I have crushed and defeated you. I need everyone to know that this is what happens when you mess with me. That I am indestructible."

He smiled. "You are my living message. Just count yourself lucky I didn't pick a worse task for you."

He stood up, and Peachey tried again to charge at him, but the drug had taken total control. He felt his muscles move, or he thought he did, but he was as still as a statue.

Buckland didn't say goodbye. He just stood up and walked out. The door jingled shut behind him.

Come on, Michael, Peachey told himself. Move.

He tried to wiggle his fingers, but the paralysis was only getting worse. They didn't budge.

Come on. You can do it.

Buckland had stranded him here for a reason. And he didn't want to be here when whoever was coming to pick him up arrived.

Move. Move, damn it!

He couldn't even let go of his cup of coffee. His fingers seemed to be glued to it, just like his forearms were glued to the table, and his feet were glued to the floor. He was a photograph instead of a man.

The door jingled again, this time more forcefully. A man in a brown coat walked in, raised a Colt .45, and pointed it at Peachey's chest. With his other hand he held up a police badge.

"I'm Detective Damien Wright," he said. "I'm arresting you for the murder of Hammond Buckland. You do not have to say anything, but it may harm your defence if you do not mention, when questioned, something which you later rely on in court. You have the right to an attorney. If you cannot afford one, one will be provided for you by the state. Put your hands on your head."

Peachey's jaw was frozen in place. His tongue was stuck to the floor of his mouth. It was hard to breathe.

"I said, put your hands on your head," Wright said, approaching slowly.

Peachey thought of the recording in his pocket, the one that implicated both him and Tania Walker. He wondered what sort of sentence he would get if he confessed and turned in Adam Keighley as well.

Presumably it would be shortened once the police realized that Buckland wasn't actually dead.

"Put your hands on your head, now!" Wright said. His gaze was cold and hard.

Peachey's fingers still wouldn't move. Gold-speckled people swept past outside the window, pockets overflowing. In a dark alcove, some children were making a small gold snowman.

He thought of the money that should have been his. He thought of the girl who'd escaped. He thought of the man who'd outsmarted him and the prison cell that would be waiting and his first-ever mission failure.

Then he thought of the imaginary movie about his life, and his frozen lips stretched into a slow, numb smile.

Maybe, he told himself, it will be made sooner than I thought.

Ash put the earphones in her ears. "Bad news, Benjamin," she said.

"I saw it on the news," he replied gloomily. "If it helps, the explosion didn't touch the helicopter you nicked. You can still use it to escape."

"That's good," she said. "But it won't be as stylish as Buckland's exit."

"Exit? You mean he's not dead?!"

"Nope," Ash said. "The bullets were blanks, and he had those things under his clothes that they use in the movies to make people look like they're getting shot."

"How did he get the blanks into the gun?"

"I have no idea. Don't know how he knew where Peachey would aim, either. But he's not here – the fake TRA guys drove him away inside the anthrax box." She sighed. "He planned the whole thing; and now we're left with nothing."

"Well, not nothing exactly," Benjamin said. "You've still got the cheque for ten grand he gave you, right?"

Ash smiled. "Yeah, that's something, I guess." She took

the envelope out of her pocket and tore it open. She was surprised to see not only a cheque, but a letter too.

Dear Ash,

By the time you read this, I will be a long way away. Now that I don't have the money the government wanted, I'm hoping there won't be anyone chasing me – but I can't guarantee that there won't still be a price on my head. It's not safe to tell you where I've gone.

You must be disappointed to see so much money slip through your fingers. You probably even know how much it was; I'm certain you found it. You and Benjamin are, after all, exceptional thieves.

I apologize for deceiving you. I first became aware of you and Benjamin when you attempted to steal a Bugatti Veyron from a friend of mine; I was fascinated, and have been keeping an eye on you ever since via several informers. The essay competition was staged to make sure I got to meet you in person before leaving the country – and before you attempted to rob me. For what it's worth, your essay really was the best.

This afternoon, I told you the truth – once you have more money than you need, you start looking for something else. You want reason, purpose, meaning.

If you had won today, before long you would have felt as empty as I do. I know you first stole out of necessity, but I also know that now you do it recreationally. Don't lose your way. Don't take from good people. The excitement will fade, leaving remorse that you will be powerless to scrub away.

I'm going to make you an offer. You've seen my world, crossed swords with killers, and lived to fight again. Now you're ready to decide.

I have in my possession a list of one hundred priceless items that have been stolen. There are paintings, musical instruments, ancient artefacts, and even human body parts on it. I've written their current hiding places, the names of their rightful owners, and their dollar value beside each one. Their original owners will pay handsome rewards for their return. Their captors will stop at nothing to keep them.

You'd be doing what you do best, but for a good cause. And very good money.

Interested?

The Source

PS I've put a small down payment in the envelope to get you started.

Completely astonished, Ash removed the cheque from the

envelope. At first she thought it was just $10,000, but then she counted the zeroes. It wasn't $96 billion, or even $200 million. But it was a start.

There was also a photograph. Buckland, smiling, with a big moustache and glasses. Ash gaped. He had been the courier on the aeroplane. The one escorting the alexandrite sculpture. She grinned.

She took the coffee voucher Buckland had offered her that morning out of her pocket. Two regular coffees, from any shop on the street.

"Hey Benjamin," she said. "Want to get a coffee with me once I'm out of here?"

"Like, a date?" he asked hopefully.

"More like a business proposal," Ash said, grinning. "But trust me, you're going to love it."

Ash and Benjamin are back in

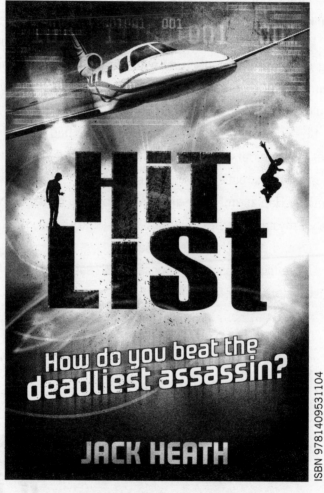

How do you beat the deadliest assassin?

JACK HEATH

Coming soon

**How do you beat the deadliest assassin
in the world...**

**And a gang of murderous mercenaries...
And a thief who can walk through walls...
And a detective with a grudge...
...when they all want to destroy you?**

Teen thieves Ash and Benjamin are suddenly top
of everyone's hit list. And when you're about to break
into the largest intelligence agency in the world to rescue
a mysterious stranger, that's a seriously dangerous
place to be.

*"Gripping to the final page. Perfect for fans of
Anthony Horowitz."* **The Sun Herald**

*"Smart, slick and explosive, this is teen crime fiction
at its best."* **Booktrade.info**

"Robin Hood on steroids."
NSW Association for Gifted & Talented Children

Acknowledgements

Special thanks to my girlfriend, Venetia, whose unconditional support made this book possible. Also to Mum, Dad and Tom, who are always there for me, reading drafts, offering encouragement, and driving me to the airport at unreasonable hours of the morning.

Thanks to Billy Griffiths for much-needed feedback on an early draft.

Thanks everyone who volunteered their names for characters – I hope those I used enjoy seeing themselves as thieves and murderers.

There's a reason I keep thanking the team at Pan Macmillan – they're awesome. They treat their readers and their writers so well. I'd like to thank Anna McFarlane, Cate Paterson, Bri Tunnicliffe, Mary Verney, Penny Mansley and Ali Lavau, who looked after me and this book. Kudos to Sue Bobbermein and Julianne Sheedy, for their amazing publicity work. And special thanks to Claire Craig, whose perfectionism and creativity has once again turned a sequence of seemingly random events into a coherent novel.

I'd like to thank all the writers who made me feel so welcome – it means a lot. Special thanks to J.C. Burke, Terry Denton, Kate Forsyth, Scot Gardner, Barry Heard, Simon Higgins, Simmone Howell, Andrew Hutchinson, Justine Larbalestier, David Levithan, Tara Moss, Matthew Reilly, James Roy, Scott Westerfeld, Lili Wilkinson, and Markus Zusak. You all give this profession a good name.

I also want to thank the many musicians I've played alongside; every writer needs a break sometimes. There are many of you, but special mentions go to Sophie Chapman, Harry Coulson, Adam Dixon, Lia McKerihan, David Mahon, Debbie Masling, Brendan Magee, Kerri Gleeson, Reuben Ingall, Paddy Quiggin, and Tracy Webster.

Thank you librarians and teachers, for putting my books in students' hands. It's an honour to be your go-to guy for reluctant readers and voracious ones alike.

Thank you to the fans, for trusting me and allowing me the

freedom to try something new. Hope you like it!

Lastly, a very special thank you to Paul Kopetko, to whom this book is dedicated. Everyone needs a friend like Paul; the tragedy is that he's one of a kind.

About the author

Jack Heath is an award-winning author of action-adventure books. He started writing his first book when he was thirteen years old and had a publishing contract for it at eighteen.

He is also the founder of New Poe, a website on which writers submit, critique, and win prizes for short stories.

When he's not writing or web-designing, Jack is performing street magic, composing film music, teaching or lecturing at schools and festivals, or playing a variety of instruments, including the piano and the bass guitar. He stoically ignores his lack of qualifications or training in any of these areas.

Jack lives in Canberra, Australia, with his girlfriend and their cat, Onyx.

jackheath.com.au

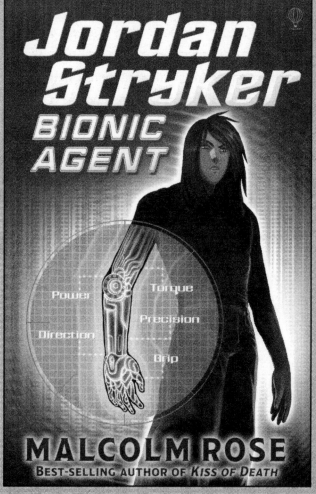

A massive explosion destroys the south-east
of England. The near lifeless body of Ben Smith
is plucked from the carnage…

Deep within the secret headquarters of the
mysterious government agency, Unit Red, Smith is rebuilt
as…Jordan Stryker. New technology gives him
unbelievable new powers, and now he has a mission:
to hunt down the perpetrators of one of the biggest
crimes ever known.

Can Jordan outwit the evil masterminds and
violent gangs who will use any means to destroy
their enemies?

**"Buzzing with the thrills and spills
of a James Bond blockbuster…"**
Lancashire Evening Post

**AND THE GRIPPING
SEQUEL IS ALSO
OUT NOW...**

ISBN 9781409509776